DISGUSTING DAVE

and the
Bucketful
of Vomit

Also by Jim Eldridge:

Disgusting Dave and the Farting Dog
Disgusting Dave and the Flesh-eating Maggots

DISGUSTING DAVE

and the Bucketful of Vomit

Jim Eldridge

Illustrated by David Millgate

A division of Hachette Children's Books

A Catalogue record for this book is available from the British Library

ISBN 978 1 444 90156 6

Typeset by Avon DataSet Ltd, Bidford on Avon, Warwickshire
Printed and bound in Great Britain by CPI Bookmarque, Croydon

The paper and board used in this paperback by Hodder Children's Books are natural
recyclable products made from wood grown in sustainable forests. The manufacturing
processes conform to the environmental regulations of the country of origin.

Hodder Children's Books
A division of Hachette Children's Books
338 Euston Road, London NW1 3BH

An Hachette UK company
www.hachette.co.uk

For Lynne,
my inspiration,
as ever

CHAPTER 1

SPLAT!!

Banger Bates suddenly leant forward and vomited, the sick splashing out of his mouth right on to our class table.

Everyone else on our table, and those around us, started to make sick noises, and go 'Yurk!' and things, and got up and moved away.

'Stop!' called out our teacher, Miss Moore.

Whether she was telling us not to move, or Banger not to vomit again, it didn't work.

SPLAT!!

Banger's mouth opened and another load of vomit poured out on to the table, and the kids who had stayed sitting now got up and ran for a place as far away from Banger as possible, yelling and screaming.

'I don't feel well!' moaned Banger. He pushed his chair back, and then fell out of it and landed on the floor, groaning.

'Keep away from the sick!' yelled Miss Moore sharply.

To be honest, she didn't really need to say it, as that's what everyone in our class was doing their best to do. Some of the kids' faces were looking distinctly white and green as they looked at the vomit splashed on the table. It's an interesting thing about vomit. I read somewhere that sick always looks as if it's got small bits of carrot in it, even if you haven't eaten carrots. I moved forward to get a better look at the sick and see if I could identify any small orange bits that might be carrots in it. As I did, Miss Moore roared out, 'Dave Dickens! Get away from that!'

I stepped back, and as I did I stepped in something wet and slippery and nearly fell over. It was more sick, but it wasn't Banger's.

Then I realised what had happened. Some of the kids had felt sick watching Banger throw up, and some of them had actually vomited right on the floor where they were standing. This only made things worse, as other kids were now turning shades of green at the sight of even more vomit on the floor, and also threw up.

FACTOID:
Vomit
You vomit when your brain senses poisons in your stomach.

'Everybody out!' shouted Miss Moore, who – I noticed – was also looking very pale about the gills.

We all headed for the door, except for Banger, who was still lying on the floor and groaning. Then he threw up again.

By now the teacher from the class next door, Mrs Walton, had turned up to see what all the shouting was about. She saw the mess on the table and the

floor, smelt the smell of vomit, and recoiled as if someone had stuffed a rotten fish under her nose.

It was then I saw my friend Suki had knelt down beside Banger and was turning him so that his face was pointing downwards.

'Suki Patel, what *are* you doing?' shouted Miss Moore.

'I'm putting him in the recovery position, miss,' said Suki. 'So he can't choke on his vomit.'

'Very good, but get away from him!' ordered

Miss Moore.

'But, miss …' protested Suki.

'I said, "Get away"!' repeated Miss Moore, firmly. 'Now!'

Suki sighed and let Banger's head go, and his face fell forward on to the floor, right into the latest pool of vomit he'd just chucked up.

I was interested to see if Banger might accidentally breathe this vomit up his nose, but before I could get a good and proper look, Mrs Walton had ushered us all out into the corridor.

The kids who'd been sick in the classroom leant against the wall looking green and miserable and did their best not to look down at where their sick had splashed on to their clothes.

My best friend, Paul, sidled up to me. 'Wow!' he said. 'That was amazing! Did you see how fast it spread?'

I noticed that Suki was looking really unhappy.

'Miss Moore shouldn't have stopped me,' she complained. 'I knew what I was doing!'

'You were really brave,' I told her. I looked at her hands, which had streaks of Banger's vomit on them. 'You deserve a medal. You saved his life.'

'Yes. I wouldn't have done what you did,' agreed Paul. 'I'd have let Banger choke.' Suki looked at him, shocked, and he hastily added, 'But only a bit. Then I'd have saved him.'

Just then, Mrs Nelson our head teacher appeared, and took charge.

'All those who've been sick, go to the medical room,' she said. 'The rest of you go with Mrs Walton to her classroom.' Turning to me, she said, 'Dave, go and see Mr Morton and tell him to bring a big bucket of hot soapy water. And disinfectant.'

CHAPTER 2

This all happened in the middle of the afternoon, so we spent the next hour being tidied up, and then Mrs Nelson gave us all a letter to take home to inform our parents that there had been some illness at school, and to watch out in case any of us showed any symptoms of sickness.

When the bell went for the end of school, Paul grabbed me.

'I've got something to show you!' he said, hardly able to contain his excitement.

Curious, I followed him to the cloakroom. He pulled out his new mobile phone. He was very proud of it. His mum had bought it for him as a present a few days before.

'Look!' he said. He clicked a button and on the

screen appeared a film of Banger throwing up in our classroom. 'Brilliant, isn't it?' he said. 'Look at the definition! It's really clear. That's because of the number of pixels on the screen.'

I wasn't impressed. Well, I was, but secretly. And I was also a bit jealous. The thing is that everyone I know seems to have a mobile phone, except me. My parents won't let me have one because my mum says that the microwaves might damage my brain while it's still growing. I don't get this because my sister, Krystal, has got a mobile phone and she's on it all the time, and she's only two years older than me, so her brain must still be growing. And loads of people in my class have them, including Banger Bates. Mind, Banger only has one brain cell, so I don't think microwaves will cause any damage to his brain. In fact, now Paul had got his phone, about the only people in our class who don't have phones are me and Suki.

The Big Thing for Paul, of course, is that he is a Science nut. Previously, his interests had been things about the universe and the planets, and science fiction, but lately he's got more interested in digital technology and communications. I know that he's always wanted a mobile phone that does all different sorts of things, like take photos and do apps and stuff, but his dad and mum haven't had the money. At least they admit it, unlike the 'It's bad for your brain' excuse from my parents. But then Paul's mum landed the job as cook at our school, and – like I say – she bought Paul this phone for his birthday.

When I say I was jealous, it wasn't really the phone I was jealous of (though it was), it was the fact that I had to wheedle and beg my parents to get me anything I *really* wanted for my birthday. What I like best as presents are things for my microscope – or even a bigger and stronger microscope! What I usually get are clothes – jumpers, shirts, socks – and now and then a book.

Anyway, Paul showed me more of the pictures he'd taken of Banger throwing up.

'I've a good mind to put them on the internet,' he said. Then he looked doubtful. 'Trouble is, Banger will trace it to me, and then he'll bash me up.'

We agreed it was an unfair world, and then we went home.

Fred, my dog, was waiting for me. He lumbered out of his kennel with a big sloppy smile on his face as he saw me walk up the front path, and – as I rubbed his head – he farted. That was the thing about Fred, and the reason he spent most of his time outside in his kennel. Fred was a serial farter.

Actually, his farts weren't as bad as they were when we first had him. Then they were so powerful that they could make a strong man faint at fifty paces. Since then I'd worked on his diet and made sure he had proper exercise, and now they were just general run of the mill farts. Because they were silent you didn't know about them until they hit your nostrils, and mostly these days you hardly noticed the smell. Now and then Fred could still produce a real powerful one that made your eyes water, but mostly they were just harmless.

FACTOID:
Farting
The main gases in human farts
are nitrogen and carbon dioxide.
Carbon dioxide is in higher quantities
in the farts of people who drink
lots of carbonated drinks.

I was just patting Fred and telling him about the day, and about Banger being sick and keeling over on the floor, when I heard a sort of vocal explosion behind me, and I knew that my big sister, Krystal, had arrived home.

Krystal is terrifying. She doesn't talk, she shouts angrily, especially to me. Like she was doing now.

'Don't you come anywhere near me! You've got the plague!' she hollered, and held up her hand towards me in a 'Halt' sign.

I stared at her, baffled. 'What do you mean?' I

asked, but as I spoke I must have moved towards her, because she let out a yell and jumped back.

'Stay away!' she shouted.

Krystal's shout had brought Mum out.

'What are you two up to?' she demanded.

'Dave's got the plague!' yelled Krystal. 'Everyone at his school has got it!'

FACTOID:
The Plague

Between 1347 and 1351 the Plague (also called the Black Death) killed 1.4 million people in England; which was one third of the population at that time. The plague was spread by fleas living on rats.

Mum let out a deep groan.

'Don't be silly,' she said. 'It's just one or two children feeling a bit ill, that's all.'

I stared at Mum, stunned. How did she know? I'd only just got home and I hadn't told her what had happened. Had Mum developed telepathic powers?

'Everyone in the school's been sick,' insisted Krystal. 'My friend Maxine told me, she had a text from her sister who's in Year 5.'

'Well, I was told by Mrs Porter, and she said it was only one or two children in Dave's class …' began Mum.

So *that* was how Mum knew!

'Dave's class!' repeated Krystal, horrified. 'So he *has* got it!'

'I haven't got anything!' I protested. 'I wasn't sick. The ones who were sick were Banger Bates, who started it, then Jenni Murray, Joey Small …' I continued counting them off on my fingers as I tried to picture them bending over and vomiting. '… Mark D'Abo, Anna Home – although she didn't really vomit as such, just dribbled a bit …'

'That's enough, Dave!' commanded Mum. 'I'm sure the scene was unpleasant enough without telling us about in it such unpleasant graphic details.'

'Actually it wasn't that bad,' I said. 'I mean, sick is natural. The interesting thing was the smell …'

'Urgh! You are disgusting!' snapped Krystal, and she stormed inside.

'Dave, you have to stop this,' said Mum firmly.

'I was just trying to be helpful,' I protested. 'I was trying to reassure Krystal that it wasn't anything really bad, so she needn't get worried.' I frowned, thoughtfully. 'Mum, have you heard that sick always has bits of carrot in it?'

Mum gave me a glare. 'That's enough!' she said. Then her tone softened. 'Actually, I need to talk to you.'

Immediately I got worried. Whenever Mum looks concerned and says something like 'I need to talk to you', it means that something bad is about to happen.

I could tell that whatever it was wasn't my fault, because then when she says 'I need to talk to you' her voice sounds like glass breaking. But when her voice goes quieter and softer, it means there is Bad News. I wondered what it was.

'We've got a visitor coming to stay for a while,' she said.

I knew what was coming next! I'd have to move out of my bedroom into the frightening attic upstairs. That always happens when people come to stay with us, and it's most unfair. No one asks Krystal to move out of her room and into the attic. Mind, that's understandable, because my sister is one of the most frightening people on the planet – and for quite a few surrounding galaxies as well – and I could imagine her reaction to being asked to move out of her room so one of our loony relatives could stay in it.

'Why is it always me who has to move out of my room?' I grumbled. 'When Gran came to stay, and then mad Aunt Dora …'

'Your Aunt Dora is not mad,' responded Mum firmly. 'And, anyway, you won't have to move out of your room.'

This perked me up. 'Oh?' I said, a bit more cheerfully.

'Yes, Kevin will be sharing your room with you while he's here.'

Kevin!

'Not … cousin Kevin?' I asked with a shudder.

'Yes,' said Mum. 'Brenda has got to go away for a couple of weeks …'

A couple of weeks? No!

Brenda is Mum's sister, and she's a single parent to my cousin Kevin, who's almost a year younger than me at ten years old. My gran says it's a pity Brenda can't find a husband. I say that as long as she's got Kevin, no one with a brain will want to move in with her.

Not that Kevin is dangerous or bad, like Banger Bates. He's … well, he causes problems. The main problem is that he watches detective shows on TV and wants to be a detective. In fact, he thinks he *is* a detective, and he spends his time going around trying to solve crimes. Even when there hasn't been a crime, Kevin digs around to try and uncover one, which is what causes the problems.

'Now, while Kevin's with us, I want you to be responsible for him,' said Mum. 'He looks up to you.'

'Only because he's shorter than me.'

'I want you to be like an older brother to him while he's here,' continued Mum. 'Keep an eye on him inside and outside school.'

Again, warning bells went off in my head.

'*Inside* school?' I echoed.

'Yes,' nodded Mum. 'Because of extenuating circumstances, Brenda being a single parent and all, Mrs Nelson has agreed that Kevin can spend the next few weeks at your school, while he's staying with us.'

'The next *few* weeks?!' I said, stunned. 'You said a *couple* of weeks. A couple is two …'

'Kevin will be here until she's ready to return,' said Mum.

Again, I got suspicious. I was starting to sound like Kevin being a detective, but this was beginning to seem to me like Kevin was going to be with us for much longer than just a few weeks.

'Return from where?' I asked.

'That's not important,' said Mum dismissively.

'Yes it is!' I insisted. 'If she's in somewhere like Australia, it could take her weeks to get back.'

'She's not in Australia.'

'Then where is she?'

'I don't wish to discuss it with you,' said Mum.

I knew what must have happened. Trying to live with Kevin had finally sent Aunt Brenda round the twist and she was locked up in a mental hospital. And the same would happen to me after a few weeks of living with Kevin and sharing my room with him!

'Your dad's gone to pick Kevin up,' said Mum. 'So you'd better get in and tidy your room before he arrives, so we can put up the camp bed in there for him.'

CHAPTER 3

Dad arrived about an hour later, bringing Kevin with him, just as Mum was preparing tea for us.

'Hello, Dave!' he greeted me cheerfully. 'I'm going to be sharing your room! It'll be great! Is that your dog in the kennel outside? I didn't know you had a dog. Is he a good guard dog?'

That gives you some idea of the kind of person Kevin is. He starts talking about one thing and then switches to talking about something else before you've had a chance to start to wonder about that first thing.

'His name's Fred ...' I began.

'He made a funny smell as we came past,' said Kevin.

'He farts,' said Krystal. 'He's a farting dog.'

'No he isn't,' I protested. 'No more than any other dog! And not as bad as Mr Smith at the corner shop!'

'That's enough,' said Mum sharply. She turned to Kevin and gave him her Welcoming Smile. 'How are you, Kevin?' she asked. 'Was your journey here all right?'

'Yes, except Uncle John parked illegally when he came to fetch me.'

We all looked at Dad, who let out a groan.

'There are double yellow lines all the way along the street outside Brenda's flat,' he complained.

'Uncle John didn't realise he was breaking the law until I pointed it out to him,' continued Kevin happily. 'He said he was allowed to park there. Luckily a traffic warden was just along the road, so I called him over to check, and he said I was right.'

Mum looked questioningly at Dad, who produced a piece of paper in a plastic bag from his pocket.

'Forty pounds parking fine,' he said gloomily.

'It's the law,' smiled Kevin. 'The fight against crime!'

I saw Dad grimace miserably, and knew he must be feeling pretty sick at having to be hospitable to this would-be crimebuster who'd just cost him forty pounds.

'Yes, well, now you're here it's time for tea,' Mum said. 'Eggs, beans and sausages. Will that be all right for you?'

'Great!' said Kevin. 'Did you know that a lot of sausages sold in this country are made from animals that have been rustled.'

'Rustled?' said Dad, puzzled.

'Stolen,' said Kevin. 'By rustlers. They steel sheep and cattle. It was in this programme I watched called *Animal Detectives...*'

'Well, I'm not eating in the same room as *him*,' snorted Krystal, pointing at me. 'He's got germs!'

'What sort of germs?' asked Kevin.

'I haven't got germs!' I protested. 'Just because someone was sick at school today ...'

'Lots of them were sick!' persisted Krystal. 'It was an epidemic!'

'Poisoning!' said Kevin, beaming. 'Fantastic! We shall find some clues and work out who the poisoner is!'

'There was no poisoner!' I told him. 'One boy got sick and him being sick made all the others start vomiting …'

'There is no need to be so graphic when we are about to eat,' Mum reprimanded me sharply.

With that, we all sat down with our tea on our laps and watched the TV while we ate, all except Krystal, who took hers upstairs to her room so she wouldn't be 'contaminated' by being near me.

Actually, Dad says it's not a very good idea to sit and eat while watching TV, especially in the early evening, because the national news is on, and it usually has pictures of people with diseases and injuries from bad accidents, and other stuff that's sure to put most people off their food. Personally, I don't mind and find this stuff fascinating because it's Science; but Dad usually puts on the local news instead because he says it's less likely to put him off his food. This time, though, he was wrong. When he changed channels to local TV, there were Banger and his dad standing outside our school gates, and Banger's dad was holding a bucket.

'My son was sick at school, and sick again when he got home,' he said. Then he held the bucket towards the camera. 'This is the evidence,' he said. 'A bucket with my son's vomit in it.'

'Urgh, that is disgusting!' went my dad.

The picture then cut to Mrs Nelson being interviewed in her office.

'In view of concerns about health and safety,' she said, 'the governors have decided the school will remain closed tomorrow while a thorough investigation is carried out.'

'Wow!' said Kevin, delighted. 'It *is* poisoning! Great! I can investigate it and unmask the criminal!'

Just then the phone rang. Mum answered it, listened for a moment or two, then said, 'Yes, thank you, Mrs Morris. We've just seen it on the TV news. I assume the school will be opened again on Wednesday?' She listened, and then said, 'Thank you for that,' and hung up. 'That was the secretary at Dave's school,' she said.

'Yes, we heard,' sighed Dad. 'So, no school tomorrow for you two.'

'But we can still start investigating, can't we?' asked Kevin.

'No!' Mum told him firmly. 'There is nothing to investigate. A boy got sick, and that's all there is to it.'

The picture on the screen cut back to Banger

and his dad. His dad was still holding the bucket towards the camera.

'My son's health has been put at risk by some sort of bug,' Mr Bates said into the camera, looking very fierce. 'We are going to demand a full public enquiry, and compensation!'

Dad reached for the remote and switched the TV off. 'I can't eat my tea with that bucket staring me in the face,' he complained.

CHAPTER 4

After tea, I put my coat on and got Fred's lead from the hook.

'Where are we going, Dave?' asked Kevin eagerly.

'*We're* not going anywhere,' I told him firmly. 'I'm taking Fred for his walk.'

'You should take Kevin with you,' said Mum. 'After all, he is your guest.'

I was tempted to say that Kevin wasn't *my* guest, he was being dumped on me like a dose of measles. But if I said that, then Mum would only get upset and tell me off. It was easier for a quiet life to agree with her. So instead I said, 'Right,' and me and Fred set off for the park with Kevin.

The walk to the park was a nightmare. All the way Kevin kept looking suspiciously at people and muttering about how most of them were suspected criminals. If you believed Kevin, then most of our town was like some Wanted area for crooks. I could understand it if we lived in a place where people walked about armed to the teeth with weapons, or sold drugs on the street corner, but nearly everybody in our area is law-abiding and looks boringly ordinary. I pointed this out to Kevin.

'Exactly!' He nodded. 'That's how clever these criminals are! They deliberately look ordinary so they don't draw attention to themselves!'

Just then we were passing old Mrs Wilson's house, and she was outside with her cats. She's got loads of cats who live in her house, and she looks after them all, even though she's in a wheelchair.

'What about Mrs Wilson?' I challenged him, giving her a wave as we passed. 'You can't say she's a criminal.'

'Why not?' retorted Kevin.

'Because she's in a wheelchair!' I said. 'And she has loads of cats to look after.'

'Just like Blofeld in James Bond!' replied Kevin. 'He was in a wheelchair in one of the films. And he had a cat.'

FACTOID:
Cats
Cats are the most popular pets in the world. However, because they breed fast and hunt successfully, there are millions of feral (or semi-wild) cats around the world – with about 60 million feral cats in the USA alone.

'But she hardly ever leaves her house!' I pointed out. 'How can she be a criminal if she's never out?'

'The internet,' Kevin said. 'Loads of criminals commit robberies these days without ever leaving their house. They do it over the internet. In fact, internet crime is the fastest growing area of crime!' He looked suspiciously at Mrs Wilson. 'And who's to say that wheelchair of hers isn't a fake?' he muttered. 'She could have rocket jets hidden in it, and machine guns.'

'And the cats?' I asked sarcastically. 'Are they criminals, too?'

'It's been known,' said Kevin. 'There was a man who trained his monkey to climb up drainpipes and be a burglar. If you can get a monkey to do it, you can get a cat to do it.'

FACTOID:
Animal Criminals
In many parts of Europe, until the 18th century, animals used to be tried for criminal offences, ranging from murder to criminal damage.

I was speechless. It was impossible to talk to him. Just then, Fred let off a fart. For a change, it was a really smelly one. It struck me that Fred was giving his opinion of Kevin.

Our time at the park was just as bad as our walk there. I was hoping that Paul or Suki might be there, to give me a chance to escape from Kevin, but I was out of luck. So I had to endure Kevin making comments about the park ranger being obviously some kind of crook, possibly selling trees and flowers to the Mafia, and some elderly man who Kevin was convinced was a drug dealer because he was wearing dark glasses. I pointed out that as he was also carrying a white stick, he might actually be blind.

After half an hour of watching Kevin hiding behind trees so he could observe the park ranger, once Fred had done his business, we set off back home again.

If this was how things were going to be with Kevin living with us, especially sharing my room, I asked him how long he was planning on staying. Actually, I didn't ask him outright, I was subtle and clever. I asked him how long his mum was going to be away.

'Two weeks,' said Kevin.

'You're sure?' I asked.

'That's what she said. She's gone away to Turkey with her new boyfriend.'

'How do you know?'

'Because I searched her bag and found the stickers for the labels with the name of the hotel and the tour operator.' He shook his head. 'She didn't tell me because she thinks I'll be upset because she knows what I think of this new boyfriend.'

'What do you think of him?' I asked.

'I think he's a serial killer,' said Kevin.

I stared at him, shocked. 'What?' I gulped.

'Yes,' said Kevin. 'He's got serial killer eyes and ears.'

'Ears?'

Kevin nodded. 'It was in this magazine I read about serial killers. They nearly all have the same shape earlobes. Brian has them.'

'Brian?'

'The new boyfriend. I warned Mum about him, but I could tell she didn't believe me. That's why I phoned the police. To protect her.'

I groaned. You can now see what I mean by Kevin causing problems.

'And what did the police do?' I asked, my heart sinking.

'They came round and took him in for questioning.'

'What?' I exclaimed. 'Just because you said he had serial killer earlobes?'

'Well, I may have said a bit more than that,' admitted Kevin. 'Like, I may have said he had a gun.'

I stared at him, shocked. 'You idiot!' I told him.

'What else could I do?' he protested. 'I was protecting my mum.'

I let out another groan. No wonder Aunt Brenda wanted to offload Kevin for a couple of weeks. The pity was, she landed him on me!

'Anyway,' continued Kevin cheerfully, 'I found a way to look after her while she's away. I sent an email to the Turkish police with his photograph and said he's a dangerous character who needs to be kept under close surveillance at all times. And I sent a message to the manager at the hotel they're staying at to make sure they keep an eye on my mum.'

'I don't think that was a nice thing to do,' I told him. 'You'll ruin your mum's holiday.'

'Not as much as Brian the serial killer could do,' said Kevin.

I shut up. There was no way of getting through to him.

CHAPTER 5

I was woken up in the middle of the night by strange noises in my room. There was someone moving about. I reached out and put on my bedside light, and saw Kevin by the window looking out through the gap in the closed curtains.

'Turn that light off!' he whispered urgently. 'They'll see me!'

I turned the light off, then asked, 'Who will?'

'The burglars!'

'What burglars?'

'The ones who prowl the streets at night looking for houses with open windows to break into,' said Kevin. 'That house opposite has one of its windows open. I'm keeping watch waiting for a burglar to try and break in, then I'm phoning

999 so they catch them.'

'That's Mr Edward's house,' I said. 'He leaves his windows open because he likes fresh air. But I wouldn't want to be the burglar who breaks into his house while he's there. He used to be in the SAS and he's got a black belt in Judo.'

FACTOID:
The SAS
SAS stands for Special Air Service. It was started by David Stirling during the Second World War to operate behind enemy lines.

'Great!' said Kevin delightedly. 'This could be really exciting!'

I let him stay, looking out into the street through the curtains, and went to back to sleep.

It felt as if I'd hardly put my head back on the pillow when I was woken up again, but this time by blue flashing lights outside and the sound of a police siren. I stumbled out of bed and staggered to the window, and tripped over Kevin, who was kneeling down, already watching.

'Ow!' I said. 'What's going on?'

'The police have turned up at that Mr Edward's house to arrest the burglars.'

I stared, shocked. 'You mean burglars actually tried to break into Mr Edward's house?' I said, stunned.

'Not exactly,' said Kevin. 'And to make sure they didn't, I phoned 999 and told them there were burglars there. The burglars won't strike now, not now they know the police are watching.'

A horrible thought struck me. 'You didn't use our phone to call 999, did you?' I asked.

'Of course not!' said Kevin. 'They'd have been able to trace the call.' He held up a mobile phone. 'I used one of my mum's. She's got three.'

I stared at him, stunned, and listened to the police banging on Mr Edward's door, and all the other doors in the street opening and closing as people

woke up and tried to find out what was going on. Having Kevin staying with us was going to be a Living Nightmare!

CHAPTER 6

Next morning, everyone was looking very sleepy at breakfast time.

'What was going on last night?' asked Dad. 'Police sirens and all that shouting at three o'clock in the morning.'

I looked at him and shrugged. 'No idea,' I said.

'Someone must have reported a burglar,' said Kevin, all innocence.

'Well, I wish the police had done it without all those sirens and such!' snapped Krystal. 'For one thing, sounding those sirens is going to tell any burglars they're coming, so they'll get away. For another, they woke me up, and I've got a Science test this morning!' She glared at me. 'We're not all lucky enough to have our school closed.'

From the kitchen we heard Mum exclaim, 'What? No!' in shocked tones. She was talking to someone on the phone and she'd obviously been told some really bad news.

Dad immediately got up and went into the kitchen, a worried expression on his face. I decided to follow and find out what was happening. There were already enough disasters happening in this house and I wanted to be prepared for any more.

Mum put down the phone as Dad came in and turned to look at him, horrified.

'That was Brenda. She's hysterical. The Turkish police have arrested Brian and are holding him for questioning.'

'Why, what's he done?' asked Dad.

'That's the point,' said Mum. 'She says he's done nothing. I've told her to get in touch with the British Consul and I'm sure they'll sort it out.'

'He must have done something,' insisted Dad. 'The police don't just take someone in for questioning for nothing.'

'Maybe it's mistaken identity,' I said. 'He might look like someone else.'

Mum glared at me. 'It's rude to listen to other people's conversations,' she said.

'Sorry,' I said. I was tempted to tell them it had all happened because of Kevin, but then I thought, a) they won't believe me; and b) even if they do, I'll get the blame for it in some way, because that's the way things work.

After breakfast, Krystal went off to school and Dad left for work.

'Right, I'm off to work as well,' said Mum. 'I've left a salad in the fridge for your lunch. Mrs Higgins next door is going to be looking after you ...'

'I'm old enough to look after myself!' I protested.

'No you're not,' said Mum firmly. 'Now, I've asked her to pop in and see how you boys are doing. If you go out, you're to tell her where you've gone, and who with.'

I groaned. This was worse than being at school.

'Right,' I said.

'And remember that you're in charge of Kevin. Don't leave him on his own.'

'Why not?' I asked.

'Because ...' began Mum. Then she stopped, and I saw that she was straining her ears to try and work out where Kevin was. I knew what was going on. She didn't want to say anything bad about Kevin, because it was likely he'd be listening somewhere. That's what Kevin does. He eavesdrops. He claims it's all part of his training to be a detective, 'gathering information' he calls it, but it's a real drag. It means everything you say is being noted down by him 'and may be used in evidence against you'.

'Because children his age aren't supposed to be left on their own,' she said. 'So, if you go out, you have to take him with you. But make sure he doesn't get into any trouble.'

And with that, she picked up her bag and left for work.

Almost as soon as she'd left the house, Kevin appeared, so I knew he'd been hanging around somewhere close by, listening.

'So, what are we going to do today, Dave?' he asked eagerly. 'What crimes are we going to solve?'

'We aren't going to be doing any crime solving of any sort!' I told him firmly. 'We're going round to my friend Paul's.'

'Great! Can we take your dog?'

'Of course I'm taking Fred,' I said. 'He needs the exercise.'

FACTOID:
Dogs as Tracking Animals
Humans have trained dogs to track and hunt with them. These include sight hounds, such as whippets and lurchers, and scent hounds, such as setters, pointers and terriers.

'And a dog is great if you're tracking a criminal,' said Kevin. 'They follow their scent! Dogs have got a fantastic sense of smell.'

Fred certainly has, I thought. But not in the way that Kevin meant.

CHAPTER 7

I went next door and told Mrs Higgins that Kevin and I had to go to the Grove Farm Estate to see my friend Paul. As Mrs Higgins was in the middle of cooking something and there was a smell of burning coming from her kitchen, she didn't seem to take much notice of me, just looked at me in a frantic sort of way and said, 'You're a good boy for letting me know,' and then ran back inside her house and began throwing pots and pans around.

When Fred, Kevin and I got to Paul's house, Paul was sitting on his front step with Suki. Suki's terrible little brother, Anwar, was lying face down on Paul's small front lawn.

'What's he doing?' I asked.

'Is he dead?' asked Kevin eagerly. 'Has he been attacked?'

Suki let out a sigh. 'His class are doing a project on worms and he's collecting them. He wants to collect the most and get a gold star.'

FACTOID:
Worms
Worms come in all sizes. Most are common earthworms, but the African giant earthworm is 6.7 metres long (22 feet) and the Nemertean sea-worm (also known as the bootlace worm) is 55 metres (180 feet) long.

I looked at Anwar, who was still lying face down on the ground.

'At least it's keeping him quiet,' I pointed out.

Anwar is six years old, and usually runs around at great speed and bumps into things and knocks them over. Furniture, people – you name it, Anwar can wreck it; and then Suki has to try and make things OK again. Me having to take care of Kevin was hard, but at least I knew I'd be getting rid of him in a couple of weeks when Aunt Brenda came back from Turkey (maybe even sooner, now her boyfriend was in jail!) but poor Suki was stuck with Anwar for years to come!

I noticed that Paul looked unhappy, so I asked him what was wrong.

'It's Banger Bates and his dad,' he groaned.

Banger and his family live just around the corner from Paul's house. Suki and her family live a few streets away on the same estate. The Bates are a nightmare family. Banger's dad is one of these characters with a shaved head and loads of tattoos and a mouthful of gold teeth, like a villain out of a film. Banger's real name is Edward, but he's called Banger because he spends most of his time banging into people and bashing them, or banging their heads. He's supposed to be the same age as me, Paul and Suki, eleven years old, which is why he's in the same class as us at school, but he looks more like he's fourteen. He's tall and tough and says he shaves but I'm not sure about that. I know he sometimes comes to school wearing a dreadful aftershave that smells like paint stripper and makes your eyes water. This is especially bad for me as we're on the same table in Miss Moore's class, because our names are near on the register: Bates and Dickens. I keep hoping that a load of new kids will come into our class, all with names beginning with C, like Clark and Custard and things, so I can be moved to another table away from him. But it never happens.

Anyway, like I say, Banger terrifies all the other kids at school, and everyone on the Grove Farm Estate is scared of his dad and the rest of the family. As Paul and his parents live so near to them, I assumed something bad had happened, like the Bateses throwing bits of old cars or dead animals into Paul's garden, or something.

'What have they been up to now?' I asked.

Paul looked at me, puzzled. 'Didn't you see them on the telly last night?' he asked.

'With the bucket of vomit?' I asked.

Paul nodded, gloomily. 'Right,' he said.

I frowned, slightly baffled. 'I don't get it,' I said. 'Did they bring it round your house afterwards and throw it at you?'

Paul looked at me as if I'd gone mad. 'No!' he said. 'Didn't you hear what they said? They were going to sue the school for compensation.'

'So?' I said.

'So they'll be saying it was something wrong with the school dinners ...'

Suddenly it hit me what Paul was getting at. 'Your mum!' I exclaimed.

'Right,' said Paul miserably.

As I mentioned earlier, Paul's mum had only just started work at our school as the cook in charge of school dinners. If the school got sued because of something she'd done wrong – or even if it wasn't her fault but the dinners were to blame for Banger being sick in any way – then she'd get the sack. What was worse, *she* might even be sued!

I shook my head at the thought and sat down on the step next to Paul and Suki. 'That's awful,' I groaned.

Paul took out his new mobile phone and looked at it sadly. 'And she spent all that money from her first pay cheque buying me this,' he said gloomily. 'I feel really guilty now.' He shook his head. 'If she loses her job, I'll have to see if I can get a refund on it.'

'Got one!' yelled Anwar, and he suddenly leapt up from the ground and rushed over to us, holding a worm between his fingers.

This caused Fred to get excited and he bounded over and joined us and started barking and licking at Anwar's hand, thinking that Anwar was holding a treat for him. Before we knew what had happened, Fred gave a suck.

'Aaargh!!' wailed Anwar unhappily. 'He's swallowed my worm!'

We all looked at Fred, who now stood smiling happily, his tongue hanging out, but with no sign of the worm. Fred had, indeed, swallowed Anwar's worm.

'Don't get so upset,' urged Suki. 'There are lots more.'

'It took me ages to get that one!' wailed Anwar miserably.

'I'll help you find some more!' offered Kevin. 'I'm a good detective! I can find anything! It's all about knowing where to look.'

Anwar stopped wailing and looked at Kevin admiringly. 'You can find worms?' he asked hoepfully.

Kevin nodded. 'Like I said, I'm a good detective.' He looked at Fred thoughtfully. 'Of course we can always wait until the dog does a poo and then find your worm in it.'

Actually, from a scientific point of view, that made sense. But then I thought of how much trouble I'd be in with Mum if Kevin came home with his fingers covered in Fred's poo. And I wasn't going to let Kevin use any of my latex gloves I always carry with me. So I said firmly, 'No. Absolutely not.'

'OK, then,' said Kevin. 'Come on, let's go find some worms.'

With that, Kevin led Anwar over to another part of Paul's garden where there was a small hedge. Suki watched them go.

'Who is that?' she asked.

'My cousin Kevin,' I said, and I explained to Paul and Suki about Kevin, and what a nightmare he was – I told them what he'd done to his mum's boyfriend, and about phoning the police to report non-existent burglars in our street.

'He's a menace!' I said.

'Yes, but he's very helpful,' said Suki, looking at where Anwar and Kevin were digging with their hands in the soil under Paul's hedge.

Paul groaned. 'What are we going to do to help my mum?' he asked mournfully.

A thought struck me. Not just any old thought, but worthy of a proper detective (not a Kevin).

'Only Banger was sick at first,' I said. 'All the other kids only started vomiting when they saw him being sick.'

'So?' asked Paul.

'I see what Dave means!' said Suki excitedly. 'If there had been anything wrong with the school dinner your mum made, then other kids would have been sick as well. And not just in our class!'

Paul brightened up. 'You're right!' he said. Then his face fell again. 'But how can we prove it? Banger's dad's lawyer will say the other kids must have been made sick by the food they ate. It's their word against my mum's.'

Then came my master-stroke!

'No,' I announced. 'We have the proof!' I pointed at Suki's shoe. 'Suki's still got some of Banger's dried vomit on the side of her shoe. I'll take a sample and examine it under my microscope, then compare it with what we had for school dinner yesterday. I bet it's different!'

FACTOID:
Vomit
Our stomach aches when we vomit because the muscles there have to work hard: the muscles in your abdomen squeeze down on your stomach to force the stuff in your stomach upwards.

Paul looked at me as if I'd gone mad. 'Yuk!!' he said. 'That is gross!'

Suki looked embarrassed. 'I thought I'd cleaned it all off my shoe,' she said uncomfortably.

'You did, most of it,' I said. 'But there's some just near the sole. That should be enough for me to see what's in it under my microscope.'

Paul looked doubtful. 'They'll just say you made it up,' he pointed out. 'How will they know it was Banger's vomit you examined? It could be just any old scrapings from a dinner plate or a dustbin. It won't be evidence.'

'It will be if we put it in a bag and sign a piece of paper saying what it is,' said Suki.

Paul shook his head. 'I can't see that working,' he sighed.

'Have you got a better idea?' I asked.

Paul thought it over. 'No,' he said.

'Right. Then that's what we'll do. Have you got any plastic bags indoors?'

'We've got some food bags in the kitchen,' said Paul.

'Great!' I said. 'Get two of those.'

'Why two?'

'So we can put some of the scrapes of vomit in one and seal it and sign it; and then we'll put some in the other so that I can look at it under my microscope,' I said.

Paul still looked doubtful.

'It could be the only way to save your mum's job,' I pointed out, 'and to stop her being sued.'

Paul nodded. 'You're right,' he said, getting up, a determined expression now on his face. 'It's time to fight back!'

CHAPTER 8

I put on a pair of latex gloves, and then I scraped
the bits of dried vomit off Suki's shoe and put it in
the two plastic bags. I always carry a packet with
lots of pairs of latex gloves in wherever I go, because
I never know when I might see a really good sample
of something I can look at under my microscope. If
it's something like vomit, or poo, or snot, or anything
that will have bacteria in it, it's important that you
make sure you don't actually come into contact
with it. Latex gloves are the best for this. They're
just the same as surgeons and doctors wear. They're
thin enough so you can feel what you're doing and
do it properly, but the latex protects you against
getting contamination from germs on your skin.
When you're handling *anything* that has bacteria or

microbes on, it's important to make sure you don't pick up an infection from it.

Once I had the samples of vomit, I set off for home with Fred on the lead and Kevin trotting along beside me.

'Those are clues, right?' he said.

'Clues?' I repeated.

'I saw you scraping something off Suki's shoe. From what I heard it must be vomit from this boy Banger. You're going to prove Paul's mum is innocent!'

'Don't you get fed up with listening to what everyone is saying?' I demanded, a bit put out. I'd thought that Kevin had been playing with Anwar, searching for worms, and all the time he'd been spying on me, Suki and Paul.

Kevin grinned. 'A good detective never rests!' he said. 'You never know when something you hear or see might be useful. So, Dave, what can I do to crack this case for you?'

'What case?'

'The Case of the Vomiting Scam. You think that this boy, Banger Bates, is using being sick to try and make money. You're going to analyse his vomit and prove it's a scam. What can I do?'

'Nothing,' I told him firmly. 'Stay out of this. Whenever you poke your nose in with your investigating, you cause trouble.'

'No I don't!'

'Yes you do. Look at what's happened to your mum's boyfriend in Turkey.'

'He's a serial killer.'

'No he's not. He's just a bloke who happens to have odd-shaped earlobes! And because of you he's in jail and your mum's miserable! And look how you woke up the whole street last night by telling the police there was a burglar!'

'Crime prevention,' intoned Kevin, 'is even more important than crime detection.'

'Well, in this case you stay out of it,' I warned him. 'I can't cope with you getting me into trouble. And when we get home, leave me alone. I have some investigating of my own to do.'

When we got back I left Kevin in the living room watching some detective show on daytime TV. I took Fred up to my room, rather than leave him downstairs, in case Kevin got it into his head to go off and chase villains, using Fred as a hunting dog.

Putting on a clean pair of gloves to make sure I didn't pick up any bacteria or contaminate the evidence, I took one of the plastic bags with the vomit from Suki's shoe in it and spread it thinly on a slide, then put it under my microscope.

FACTOID:
Microscopes
Microscopes come in two main types: optical and electron. The optical microscope is the oldest type and was invented in about 1590. The first electron microscope was made in Russia in the 1930s.

My microscope is my favourite thing in the whole world. It's wonderful what you can find out about things when you look at them enlarged hundreds of times. You can see the way they are made, and all the different things they are made of. What I'd really like is one of those really powerful electron microscopes that magnify about a million times, and you can see things as small as a fly's intestines. But my microscope is still pretty good. I was able to see the different things that were in the sample of vomit. It looked pretty clean. Well, as clean as vomit can be. There didn't appear to be many germs moving about in it, and if there was something in it causing people to be sick, I'd have expected to see moving germs.

I then took some of the vomit and did some other tests with it. I put some of it on strips of litmus paper to test whether it was acidic, alkaline or neutral.

Most vomit is acidic. That's because it's got a chemical called bile in it, and bile is strong acid. That's how we digest food. In fact, the human stomach makes acid strong enough to dissolve a bone in just a few hours. Because this acid is so strong, our brains makes us dribble before we vomit, so that our teeth are protected against the strong acid by the wet dribble.

Banger's vomit from Suki's shoe was definitely acidic, but that's what I expected. What I hadn't expected was to find bits of minced-up fat and gristle in the vomit, because Mrs Nelson had bought in a healthy eating menu at school, and processed meats were banned from our school dinners.

FACTOID:
Unhealthy eating
In the 21st century there has been a massive increase in children being obese. Many experts blame sugar-laden soft drinks and the increased eating of fast foods, especially those high in sugar and fats.

The thing is with vomit that if you throw up

soon after eating something, most of the stuff in the vomit looks the same as when you ate it. But if it's been in your stomach for hours and hours, that's when the acids in your stomach turn it into a slimy mess that's all one colour and is turned into poo as it's pushed through your intestines.

The fact that these bits of gristle and fat were still much the same as when Banger had put them in his mouth showed they hadn't been in his stomach for long before he threw up. But where had they come from? What had he eaten?

FACTOID:
Digestion
Fat is hard to digest. It congeals into lumps in your insides and needs a very strong chemical called bile to dissolve it. Bile comes from your gall bladder.

Perhaps all this thinking about digestion and poo had set my own body thinking on its own, because

I realised I needed to go to the loo.

As I came out of the bathroom, Krystal came up the stairs, obviously just home from school. One look at the expression on her face sent out warning signs. Not just to me, even Fred could tell by the way she moved and glared that she was in a very bad mood indeed, and he edged away, as if he was trying to hide from her, which just shows how intelligent some dogs are.

Krystal stopped at the top of the stairs and snarled at me. 'If you even speak to me I shall kill you! I shall tear your head off and use it as a football.' Then she turned to Fred and said, 'And that goes for you too, farting dog!'

With that she stormed into her room and slammed the door.

Fred and I looked at one another, puzzled and alarmed. Even though Fred doesn't understand the finer points of English, he understands body language and voice tones, and he knew that Krystal was in an even more dangerous mood than usual.

I noticed that Fred had moved so that he was now hiding behind me, just in case Krystal came back out of her room. Well, hiding as much as a dog can.

I decided it was a good idea to head downstairs to be away from Krystal in case her head exploded with all that anger and blew up my room as well as hers. Mum was just coming in as Fred and I reached the bottom of the stairs.

'Ah, Dave,' she said. 'Good. Can you run an errand for me? I forgot to get any bread. Can you get a loaf from the corner shop?'

'No problem,' I said.

'I'm only doing sandwiches,' she said. 'Just enough for you, me and Kevin. Krystal's going to Shelly's for tea.'

I looked at her puzzled. 'No she isn't,' I said. 'She's upstairs in her room.'

Mum frowned. Then she called upstairs, 'Krystal!'

There was no answer, so Mum went up and knocked on Krystal's door, and I heard my sister grunt, 'What?'

Mum opened Krystal's door and said, 'I thought you were going round to Shelly's for tea.'

That was as far as she got, then she was cut off by Krystal shouting: 'I never want to hear that cow's name ever again!'

'Krystal!' said Mum, shocked.

'Never ever!' emphasised Krystal. And then she burst into tears and slammed her door shut.

Mum came down the stairs looking shaken. 'What's up with Krystal?' she asked. 'What have you done?'

'Me?' I said, shocked. 'It's nothing to do with me! It's something to do with Shelly.'

Mum looked worried. 'I wouldn't have thought that Krystal and Shelly would ever have a row,' she said. 'They've been best friends since they were tiny.' She looked at me accusingly. 'Are you sure you haven't done anything to upset them?'

'Nothing!' I told her, indignantly. 'I only saw Krystal for a few seconds just now, when she threatened to kill me and Fred.'

'You're exaggerating,' said Mum dismissively, once again taking my mad sister's side. She frowned thoughtfully. 'Maybe it's something that Kevin's done?'

Kevin! A sudden shock struck me – I hadn't seen Kevin for ages! I'd been so wrapped up in examining the vomit I'd forgotten all about him.

'Where is Kevin?' asked Mum.

'He's in the … er …' I threw a quick glance into the living room, but Kevin wasn't there. I strained my ears towards the kitchen, but there was no sound from it. He wasn't there, either. Then I realised what must have happened: he'd gone off somewhere on his own, detecting, and causing chaos. In which case I'd get in big trouble with my mum for not keeping an eye on him.

'He's … er … in my room,' I lied. Then I called upstairs towards my door, 'Mum's home, Kevin! I'm just going round the shop for some bread. Do you want to come?'

There was silence. I turned to Mum and said,

'I expect he's reading one of his detective stories.' I gave her a reassuring smile that everything was all right.

Mum didn't look convinced. 'I wish I knew what's gone wrong between Krystal and Shelly,' she muttered.

I held out my hand for the money for the bread, mainly because I was eager to get away as fast as I could before Mum started asking more questions about Kevin. She was holding me responsible for him, and if he'd vanished and started causing chaos and trouble all over town, then I'd be in big trouble. I had to find him, and fast!

Mum gave me some money.

'I'll just get Fred's lead from my room,' I said, and hurried upstairs.

'But …' began Mum.

I rushed into my room and looked around for something of Kevin's, something that would have his scent on it. I picked up a pair of his underpants he'd thrown on the floor and stuffed them into my pocket, then ran downstairs again.

'Silly me,' I said. 'I forgot that Fred's lead is on the hook by the back door.'

'That's what I was trying to tell you,' said Mum.

'Sorry,' I apologised.

I slipped Fred's lead on him, and hurried out, as Mum called, 'Don't be long!'

I let out a silent groan to myself. Kevin had gone missing and could be anywhere, and I had hardly any time to find him, otherwise I was going to be in Big Big Trouble!

CHAPTER 9

As soon as we were out of sight of the house, I took Kevin's underpants from my pocket and held them to Fred's nose.

'Find him, Fred!' I urged.

FACTOID:
Scent

Human scent is given off by different parts of the body: the skin (through sweat glands) and the air we breathe out (that mixes scents from our lungs and our stomachs). Two particular areas that give off strong smells are under our arms and our genital area.

I hoped that Kevin was right about Fred being

able to follow a scent. These underpants certainly were smelly enough for Fred to get a whiff of Kevin's bodily odours.

Fred looked at me with a puzzled expression on his face as if he didn't know why I was stuffing a pair of smelly underpants at his nostrils.

'Go on, Fred!' I said again, more urgently. 'Find Kevin!'

And then it was almost as if Fred's brain made a leap of understanding, because he gave a big sniff at the underpants, and then a tug that almost

pulled his lead out of my hand, and we were on the hunt!

This is great! I thought. Fred is being a real hunting dog, tracking someone down!

With Fred straining at his lead, we rushed down the street, then another street, then another. All the time Fred kept his nose close to the pavement, sniffing away as he hurried along, hot on Kevin's trail!

Soon we'd reached the industrial estate with all the factories and stuff. Fred continued hurrying along, getting faster now, and letting off the occasional fart because he was so excited at the chase. There was now a strong smell in the air: a mixture of methane and rotting vegetation, like an overripe compost heap in its early stages. Proper compost that's been rotting for ages doesn't smell at all. Well, it does have a bit of an earthy smell, but that's all. It's only fresh stuff that's waiting to be composted that has a bad smell. I know this because Miss Moore took our class to a farm and showed us the compost heaps and the worm bins, where worms turn old rotten food into good soil; and the older the compost was, the less it smelt. The smell I was getting now was definitely of fresh compost. It was more than that, it was stuff waiting to be got ready to be turned into compost, so it smelt pretty rotten. But what puzzled me was what this had got to do with finding Kevin.

Suddenly, Fred stopped. He turned to look at me, a proud smile on his face and his tail wagging.

I was baffled. There was no sign of Kevin anywhere. Instead, there was a sign that said, *Council Garden Waste Recycling Depot.* What on earth did Kevin's dirty underpants have to do with garden waste? Nothing, that's what! Fred had failed me!

'You idiot dog!' I snapped at him.

Fred's face fell and his tail stopped wagging. He could tell I was angry with him, but he didn't know why. And then, when I thought about it, I realised that Fred hadn't done anything wrong. Kevin's underpants smelt like a load of garden waste. Actually, they smelt a lot worse, but I guess that garden waste was the nearest Fred could work out. I felt really guilty.

'I'm sorry, Fred,' I apologised, and rubbed his ears. 'It wasn't your fault.'

Fred gave a half-smile and wagged his tail again, but not so perkily as usual. He could tell that I wasn't happy.

I let out a heavy groan. 'We'll never find Kevin!' I moaned. 'The police will have to be called out and they'll search for him, and find him lost somewhere miles away! I'll be in trouble for years! Dad will stop my pocket money and Mum will never talk to me again! My life is ruined!'

'Hello, Dave!' said a cheerful voice just behind me. Kevin!

I turned round, and there was my cousin.

'Why … where … what are you doing here?' I exploded.

'You told me to stay out of what you were doing, so I did. I went detecting on my own.' He smiled smugly. 'I have information. We can crack this case!'

I stared at him, still stunned. 'Where have you been?'

'The Bates' house,' he said.

I felt myself give a shudder. Kevin had been at Banger's house!

'Doing what?!' I demanded, having visions of Banger coming round to our house and taking revenge on me for whatever dreadful things it was that Kevin had done to him and his house.

Kevin grinned. 'I'll tell you when we get back home,' he said. He rubbed his stomach. 'It must be tea-time. I'm feeling hungry. What are we having for tea?'

That was when I remembered I still hadn't got the bread for Mum.

'Nothing, if I don't get to the shop,' I said, hurrying off, hauling Fred along. 'Now stay with me and don't go off doing any detecting on the way. And, if Mum asks, you came with me to get the bread.'

Kevin winked. 'I get it, Dave!' he said. 'An alibi!'

CHAPTER 10

Mum was waiting for us when I got home, a look of thunder on her face. She looked pointedly at her watch.

'Where have you been?' she demanded.

'Er ...' I began.

The trouble is I can't lie. Well, I do, but I'm hardly ever successful at it. When I lie, the tips of my ears go red and I get all tongue-tied, because I'm sure the person I'm talking to knows I'm lying and is just waiting for me to say the wrong thing so they can pounce and say 'A-ha! Got you!', just like one of Kevin's favourite detectives.

'I asked Dave if he'd show me the safest way home,' Kevin suddenly chipped in. 'The trouble is there are so many roads to cross between here and the shop and lots of them are unsafe for children. I told Dave that it's illegal for children to be out crossing those sort of roads on their own, so he showed me where the pedestrian crossings were so we could walk safely.'

FACTOID:
Pedestrian Crossings and Jaywalking
In the USA, crossing a busy road without using a pedestrian crossing is called 'jaywalking', and is a crime. Fines vary from state to state, and can be from $1 to $750.

Mum gaped at Kevin, bewildered. 'You're joking!' she said, stunned.

'Not at all!' said Kevin firmly. 'If you like I can call the police and they'll tell you what I just said is true.' And he pulled out his mobile phone.

'No, no!' said Mum hastily. Turning back to me, she said, 'That was very good of you, Dave, to be so kind and caring with your cousin.'

'Yes, he is,' said Kevin. 'I like staying with Dave. Maybe I can stay for longer than just two weeks?'

I felt my heart sink.

'Er … we'll talk about that later,' said Mum. 'Now put that dog in his kennel and wash your hands and I'll make tea.'

I put Fred on his chain by his kennel and then walked into the house, where Kevin was waiting for me. He grinned.

'Alibi!' He chuckled. 'Good, eh!'

We went upstairs to my room. Krystal was still in her room by the sound of it. Her door was shut but I could hear her talking on her mobile to one of her friends. It wasn't Shelly, because I could hear her having a go at Shelly: 'Shelly's a cow!' I heard her say. 'Shelly's a traitor!'

Listening to her, I could tell that Shelly was definitely out of favour, but at least it was safe for me to go into my room without Krystal coming in and killing me right at this particular moment.

Once we were in my room, I turned to Kevin. 'What were you doing at Banger's house?' I demanded.

'Spying on him,' admitted Kevin cheerfully. 'Getting evidence. He's got a stalker.'

I looked at him, bewildered. 'A what?'

'A stalker,' he repeated. 'Some girl. She was hanging around outside his house. Then she went up to the door and asked Banger for his autograph. After he gave it to her, she hung around a bit more, and then went away.'

FACTOID:
Autographs
The proper name for the hobby of collecting autographs is philology.

My head was reeling. Someone asking Banger for his autograph?! Banger could hardly write!

'Who was this girl?' I asked, still shocked that any girl would want to come within fifty metres of Banger voluntarily.

With uncanny detective-like style, Kevin described the girl in detail: blonde hair, a kind of vacant expression but with a happy smile stuck on it. He described the colour of her eyes, the clothes she'd been wearing, and suddenly I knew who it was.

'Shelly!' I burst out, then I hastily shut up and cast a frightened look towards my door in case Krystal had heard me.

'Shelly?' asked Kevin.

I nodded. 'My sister's best friend,' I told him. 'The one she's calling all sorts of names right now.' I looked at Kevin, bewildered. 'But why did she want Banger's autograph?'

'Because she'd seen him on the TV the night before,' said Kevin. 'I heard her tell him. She said she thought he was hunky.'

Hunky? I'd heard plenty of words used to describe Banger: thick, ugly, terrifying, gross, smelly, a bully, but never 'hunky'.

A thought struck me. 'Wait here,' I told Kevin. 'Don't make a noise.'

I crept out of my room and put my ear to Krystal's door. She was still on the phone to her friend, although her voice was quieter now.

'She says she's fallen for the most hunky boy in the world,' Krystal was telling her. 'She says he's rough and rugged. I was supposed to go round to her place after school but she went off to stand outside his house. She is a moron and I hate her!'

I crept back into my room.

Rugged? Banger?

At least I now knew why Krystal was behaving the way she was. It's always puzzled me why some people are attracted to others. The most unlikely people end up together. You see it on the news: some man with a face like a dog's bum has all these attractive women chasing after him. Mind, usually that's because he's rich or a film star, or something. But now and then it's because they say he's got 'animal magnetism'.

Despite all that, it threw me that anyone would find Banger attractive and chase after him. The only thing I could imagine being attracted to Banger was a swarm of flies.

'Apart from the fact that this girl fancies him, what else did you find out?' I asked him, reluctantly. I didn't want to encourage him doing his pretending to be a detective, but at the same time I wanted to know what was going on.

'Not a lot yet,' said Kevin. 'Keeping a subject under observation can be a long process. Sometimes it means infiltrating their company and gaining their confidence. That's what the best spies do.'

I shook my head. 'You don't want to do anything like that,' I said. 'Banger Bates is dangerous, and you'll get in trouble if you start hanging around with him.' Then I looked at Kevin again. 'He wouldn't let you hang around him, anyway. He doesn't hang around with little kids. The gang of bullies he's part of are all older than him.'

Kevin smiled. 'That's not a problem,' he said

confidently. 'There are ways to get on the inside.'

The smug smile he gave me sent a shiver down my spine. I wondered what dreadful plan he was up to. Anyone who could have his mum's boyfriend arrested in a foreign country was capable of anything. And my big worry was that, whatever he got up to, it would be me who'd get the blame!

'Now listen,' I told him firmly. 'Leave this alone! *I'm* looking into it. You stay out of it. You'll only make things worse.'

I saw from the expression on his face that Kevin was about to make a protest, but then he changed his mind.

He smiled and nodded. 'All right, Dave,' he said.

Just then Mum called out from downstairs, 'Tea's ready!'

'Great!' said Kevin, and he hurried out of the room as if he hadn't eaten for days.

I stayed behind and thought. I didn't like the easy way that Kevin had said he'd stop his investigations.

It had been *too* easy. Kevin was planning on getting up to something … but what?

Then I felt my stomach rumble, and realised I was hungry, too. So I went downstairs.

CHAPTER 11

That evening Mum got a phone call from Mrs Nelson to say that the school was definitely opening again tomorrow, so the next day I set off for school. I said goodbye to Fred, gave him a pat on the head and a biscuit, and off I went with Kevin in tow.

The walk to school wasn't too bad because Kevin didn't follow anyone or spy on them, but instead kept up a constant stream of talk about his favourite TV detectives, so I was able to ignore him and just concentrate on my own thoughts, especially the puzzle about the bits of fat and gristle in Banger's vomit. But I thought I had the answer to that, and it could save Paul's mum's job!

The first thing I had to do when I got to school was take Kevin to Mrs Nelson's office so she could sort out which class he was going to be in while he was at the school, which turned out to be Miss Polska's, Class 5P.

As soon as I'd done that, I hurried off to look for Paul. He was talking to Suki in the playground. Or, rather, he was trying to talk to Suki, but her attention was on trying to stop Anwar getting into a fight with another little boy in his class.

'Come on, Merson!' Anwar was challenging, holding up both his fists to the other boy.

'Stop that, Anwar!' said Suki. 'Fighting is wrong!'

'I can take you with one hand tied behind my back!' spat back the other little kid at Anwar. 'Both hands! Both hands and a foot!'

'Stop it!' said Suki. Then she turned on the other little boy. 'If you don't stop this I'll tell Mrs Nelson!'

This made the other little boy hesitate. When Mrs Nelson gets angry it's enough to frighten strong men. All right, she's not as bad as my sister or my gran, but she's still pretty frightening.

'Huh!' he said at last. And then he went off.

Anwar went to rush off after him, but Suki had a firm grip on his coat collar that stopped him going anywhere.

'What's all that about?' I asked.

'I support Manchester United and Steven supports Liverpool,' said Anwar. 'We hate each other.'

I looked at Suki and gave a helpless shrug. When there's football rivalry, there's nothing you can do about it.

Just then the bell went for us all to line up in our classes so our teachers could take us in, so Suki had to let Anwar go. Immediately, Anwar rushed over to the other little kid – Steven Merson – and they started setting about each other, but stopped when their teacher, Miss Walcott, shouted at them.

As Paul, Suki and I headed to where our class was lining up, ready for Miss Moore to take us in, I told them what I'd discovered in Banger's vomit.

'Gristle and fat!' I said, proudly.

Paul didn't look impressed. 'So?' he said.

Suki got it, though. Her face lit up. 'Mrs Nelson

'doesn't allow processed meats in our dinners,' she said.

'Exactly!' I said. 'Which means that whatever made Banger sick, it wasn't a school dinner! I bet it was something like a burger or a kebab, which he got off a van outside.'

'Yes!' said Suki. 'Now I come to think of it, I didn't see Banger in the dining hall at lunchtime.'

Paul stared at us, and a happy smile began to form on his face.

'Dave!' he said. 'You are brilliant!'

'Actually, it was my microscope that gave me the answer,' I told him, doing my best to look modest, but I was pretty proud at hearing him describe me as brilliant.

'But we have to prove it,' said Paul.

'We can do that because I've got the other sample of Banger's vomit in that other plastic bag, sealed and signed with our names,' I told him. 'If he threatens to sue the school and your mum, we produce that as evidence.'

'Brilliant!' said Paul again.

'Have you got the vomit somewhere safe?' asked Suki.

I nodded. 'It's in a cardboard box at the bottom of my wardrobe,' I said.

Just then Miss Moore arrived and told us all to keep quiet and go in. As we walked into school behind her, I felt like I was almost bursting with pride. With my scientific equipment and skills, and my brain, I had proved that Banger hadn't been made sick by the dinner at school. I decided that after school I'd tell Kevin about my great triumph. That would show him who the real detective was our family. It was me!

FACTOID:
Police and Detectives
The Metropolitan Police of London were formed in 1829. The detective section (CID) was set up in 1878.

CHAPTER 12

Nothing much happened at school during the morning. Banger Bates was late, he didn't come to school until just before morning breaktime. His excuse was that he thought he felt a bit sick again, but then he found out he was all right after all. As excuses went, it wasn't much, but then it was nice and simple and impossible to prove that Banger was lying, which I was sure he was. Some people try too hard when they come up with excuses about why they're late for school, and the cleverer they think they're being, the more likely they are to be found out. Years ago I found this book with a list of excuses for getting out of doing things like chores at home, and there was a whole section on reasons for being late for school. They included:

- Signals from space satellites have been interfering with my digital alarm clock, so it went off an hour late.

- I was here much earlier, but no one else was, so I went home again thinking school had been cancelled.

- We were burgled last night and I had to wait for the police to come to give my statement.

- The bus driver collapsed at the wheel and we had to wait for another bus.

- I was doing my Biology project and wanted to see if I could wake up automatically at 7.30. I couldn't.

And a whole load of others. I tried some of them out on Miss Walcot, who was my teacher at the time, but she checked up on them and found out I was lying, and I got into Big Trouble. That's why I say Banger's excuse of just feeling a bit sick, and then being all right, is the best sort. Trying to be too clever can backfire.

Morning break and lunchtime were quiet, too.

For once, Anwar didn't get into trouble like he usually does. In fact, I saw that Kevin was talking to him, and Anwar was nodding as he listened. That was unusual because Anwar never usually listens, he just runs around and knocks into things. Just in case Kevin was planning something that might cause trouble, I thought about going over and asking them what they were talking about, but then I decided against it because it was bound to be about detectives, and Kevin would just bore the feet off me by listing all his favourite detectives.

Everything changed soon after lunch.

We were sitting in our classroom, while Miss Moore talked to us about the Ancient Egyptians, when suddenly there were sounds of panic and commotion in the corridor outside our room. Immediately, Banger jumped up from our table and ran to the door and opened it to find out what was going on, but Miss Moore barked at him, 'Edward Bates! Sit down at once!'

She strode to the door, turned to us, and said, 'You

are all to stay in your seats while I am out of the room!' Then she disappeared towards where the sounds of panic were coming from, which was Miss Walcott's room, and the class that Anwar was in. Immediately, I got suspicious. Kevin, who had got his mum's boyfriend arrested in Turkey, and also woke up our street in the middle of the night by calling 999, had been seen by me talking to Anwar at lunchtime. Now Anwar's class was in uproar. The two had to be connected.

Of course, once Miss Moore had left the room, everyone in our class, including me, got up and rushed for the door to see what was going on. I looked along the corridor and saw Miss Walcott come out of her room with three little kids following her, all looking pretty ill.

I heard Miss Moore say, 'Don't worry, Miss Walcott, I'll look after your class,' and then she went into Miss Walcott's room and we heard her shout, 'Don't tread in it! All of you, sit down!'

A second later she reappeared from Miss Walcott's

room and looked towards us. Immediately, everyone ducked into our room and headed back to their seats. Everyone, that is, except me. I was unlucky enough to be nearest the door and I couldn't battle my way through the crowd of kids quickly enough.

'Dave Dickens!' called Miss Moore.

This is it, I moaned to myself. Caught! Now I'm in trouble.

I shuffled slowly along the corridor towards where Miss Moore was waiting, but instead off telling me off, Miss Moore had a job for me.

'Dave, go and find Mr Morton and get him to bring his mop and bucket and some disinfectant. Tell him some children have been sick.'

FACTOID:
Disinfectant
Disinfectants must be used with care as they are potentially harmful to humans and animals. Often the bacteria they are supposed to kill can develop a resistance to a particular type of disinfectant.

I looked into the classroom. Sure enough, there were three puddles of vomit on the floor, and the rest of the class were all standing by the side of the room so that none of them would tread in it. I noticed that even Anwar was staying where he was at the side of the room, pressed against the wall. That's the way it is with a teacher like Miss Moore; if she tells you to do something, you do it.

'Stop looking at it, Dave, and go and get Mr Morton!' snapped Miss Moore.

'Yes, miss,' I said, and I hurried off.

Mr Morton was sitting in his caretaker's office reading his paper. He must have heard all the commotion but I reckon he'd chosen to stay where he was, in case he had to do something. Like he had to now.

I told him about the kids being sick. He groaned and picked up his mop and bucket and a bottle of disinfectant and trudged unhappily off. I followed him. As I did so, my mind was in a whirl.

There was something not right about this. Three

little kids being sick, just days after kids had been sick in our class. It couldn't be just a coincidence. I was convinced that Kevin was behind it in some way, and it was quite likely something to do with Anwar too, but I couldn't work out what was going on.

The answer would be in the sick. I needed to get samples and examine them under my microscope and find out what the connection was between them. See if the sick had any of the ingredients of today's school dinner in them. And I had to do that before Mr Morton cleaned it up. But if I tried to sneak into the room, Miss Moore would order me out before I had a chance to get some samples of sick. And I didn't have my latex gloves on me! They were in my bag in class. I had to do something!

CHAPTER 13

Suddenly I had an idea.

I hurried back into Mr Morton's room. Sure enough, there was a box with latex gloves on it on one of the shelves. I grabbed a pair and pulled them on, then hurried back out into the corridor. Mr Morton was still walking along very slowly, not at all keen to tackle the pools of vomit.

'Mr Morton!' I called.

He stopped and looked at me.

'Can I carry your mop for you?' I offered.

He hesitated, then he nodded and gave it to me. 'Only be careful with it,' he said. 'That's school property, that is.'

I took the mop. Now I had my excuse for getting into Miss Walcott's classroom.

I followed Mr Morton into Miss Walcott's room, carrying the mop. Anwar and the other kids stayed by the wall, while Miss Moore started telling Mr Morton what he had to do. This has often struck me as a strange thing about teachers: they insist on giving orders to people when it's obvious to even the brain-dead what has to be done. There were three pools of sick on the floor. Mr Morton had a mop and bucket and a bottle of disinfectant. He didn't need to be a genius to work out what he had to do, but Miss Moore insisted on giving him a lecture about filling up his bucket with water from the class sink and then cleaning up the sick.

While she was doing that, I grabbed the opportunity to see if there was anything I could use to put some of the sick into. I needed enough containers to collect three separate samples. Then I saw some small plastic pots with screw-top lids on Miss Walcott's desk, which had things like paperclips and gold stars in. While Miss Moore was still giving Mr Morton instructions on How To Mop Up Sick, I grabbed three of the pots and emptied their contents on to Miss Walcott's desk, and then bent down and started scooping up the different sick into the pots using a paintbrush.

FACTOID:
Vomit
In your brain is a part called 'the vomit centre'. It is this that tells your body to lean forward and open your mouth just before you throw up.

I'd just finished, when Miss Moore spotted me and snapped, 'Dave! What do you think you're doing?'

'I dropped something, miss!' I said.

'Well, get up at once and get back to class!'

Just then Miss Walcott reappeared, but without the three sick little kids. She'd obviously left them in the medical room.

'I'm back, Miss Moore,' she said.

I noticed she looked really really pale. Miss Walcott always looked pale, even by everyday standards, like she'd been kept in a cupboard all her life and hadn't ever seen the light of day. But today she looked even paler than that.

'Are the children all right?' asked Miss Moore.

'Yes,' said Miss Walcott. 'Mrs Hurst is looking after them and Mrs Nelson's phoned their parents.'

'Good,' said Miss Moore. 'Turning to me, she said, 'Right, Dave. Let's get back to our classroom.'

Luckily, during the exchange between her and Miss Walcott, I'd managed to snaffle a bag to put the three plastic pots of sick in, so I followed Miss Moore back to our class, hiding the bag with the pots of sick in behind my back.

Everyone was sitting in their seats as we came back in, but only because the lookout had seen Miss Moore coming and everyone had rushed back to their tables just before she walked in.

'Right,' announced Miss Moore. 'The excitement is over for today. Now, we return to our worksheets and the Ancient Egyptians.'

FACTOID:
Ancient Egyptians

The Ancient Egyptians mummified their dead rulers by taking out all the internal organs that could go rotten (stomach, liver, intestines, lungs) and then putting the body in a kind of salt for forty days before wrapping the body in layers of bandages sealed with resin.

There was nothing more that happened that was exciting that day. When the bell went for the end of school, Paul and Suki grabbed me as we left our classroom.

'Was it really more kids being sick?' asked Paul.

'Yes,' I told him.

'I don't understand it,' said Suki. 'Why would that happen again?'

'I don't know,' I admitted. 'But it wouldn't surprise me to find out that my cousin Kevin had something to do with it.'

'What? Why?' asked Suki.

'Because I saw him talking to your brother at lunchtime, and it was after that the kids were sick. And Anwar is in Miss Walcott's class.'

Suki shook her head firmly. 'Anwar would never do anything really wrong like make people sick,' she said.

'He may not have known what he was doing,' I pointed out. 'Kevin could have fooled Anwar into giving the kids some stuff that made them sick. Sick sweets from a joke shop, that sort of thing.'

'Would Kevin do that sort of thing?' asked Paul.

'He got his mum's boyfriend arrested,' I reminded them. 'Kevin is capable of anything.'

Suki looked worried. 'I'll talk to Anwar,' she said.

'I'll come with you,' I said.

We hurried towards Miss Walcott's class. Paul came too.

'I hope it was something to do with Kevin and Anwar,' he said. 'Otherwise my mum might get blamed for it again.'

Anwar was putting on his coat as we arrived at his classroom. 'Hello, Suki!' he said cheerfully. 'Did you hear about the kids in our class being sick! It was massive!'

Suki eyed him with a firm glance. 'Anwar, did you give anything to them to make them sick?' she demanded.

Anwar stared back at her. 'No!' he said, indignant. 'Why would I do something like that?'

'Because my cousin Kevin might have asked you to,' I said.

Anwar shook his head. 'No, he didn't,' he said. 'And even if he did, I wouldn't have done that.'

'Then what was he talking to you about?' I asked.

At that, Anwar looked uncomfortable. 'When?' he asked.

'At morning break,' I said. 'And at lunchtime.'

Anwar hung his head and mumbled something.

'What?' I asked him.

'Anwar, speak up,' said Suki.

Anwar looked up. 'I'm not allowed to say,' he said.

'It's a secret. Top secret.'

Me, Paul and Suki exchanged worried looks. There was definitely something going on here, and Kevin and Anwar were involved. The question was, did it have anything to do with the little kids being sick?

'I'll go and talk to Kevin,' I said. 'I'll find out what's going on.'

I hurried along to Miss Polska's classroom, but all the kids had gone. Miss Polska was still in her room, writing in her mark book.

'Excuse me, Miss Polska,' I said, 'but do you know where my cousin Kevin is?'

She gave a puzzled little frown and said, 'I thought he was with you. He said he was going to find you.'

I felt a sick feeling in my stomach. This was all I needed, for Kevin to go home alone without me. If that happened and Mum found out, I'd get really told off for letting him walk home unattended.

I rushed back to our classroom in case Kevin was there, waiting for me, but he wasn't. I then went from room to room, checking the corridor and all the cupboards in case Kevin was doing his spy thing and hiding, watching people. He wasn't. He was nowhere to be found. He'd gone, and I was in Big Trouble.

CHAPTER 14

I hurried home, the samples of vomit in my bag. With luck I'd be back not long after Kevin got there, and I could maybe pretend that I'd been following him home so he wasn't ever on his own. But I didn't have any luck. Or, rather, I did, but it was bad luck.

As I turned the corner away from our school, I ran straight into three of the boys from Banger's gang. Literally. Because I was in a rush I ran round the corner, and straight into this thug called Pod.

'Ow!' he said. Then he grabbed me by the ear. 'Where d'you think you're going, Dickens?!' he snapped.

'Home,' I said.

'No you're not,' he said. He turned to the two boys with him and asked, 'What do you think, mates?'

The other two were Jaz and Mick. All three of them are older than me and Banger, and at the High School, but for some reason they hang around with Banger and treat him as their leader. I don't understand it. Banger is younger than them. I was about to add, 'and more stupid than them', but when I think about it, it's not the case. Pod, Mick and Jaz are just as stupid as Banger. They are also just as terrifying.

Jaz grinned.

'I think we ought to take a look at what he's got in his bag,' he said.

'Good idea!' said Pod. And before I could stop him, he'd snatched my bag off me and opened it. 'Well, well, what have we got here!' he said, his eyes sparkling, and he pulled out one of the small plastic pots of vomit.

'Let's have one,' grunted Mick, and he took out

another. Jaz lifted out the final one.

'What's this?' demanded Pod.

'It's sick,' I said. 'Vomit.'

Pod looked at the plastic pot, gave it a shake, and saw the yellowy sludge inside move a bit.

'Oh yeah, I'm bound to fall for that one!' He laughed scornfully. 'You must think I'm stupid or something!'

'Yeh,' chuckled Jaz, 'like anyone would be carrying around three pots of sick in his bag!'

And they all laughed.

'This is some kind of sweet drink that Dickens here is too selfish to want to share with his pals. Well, I don't call that friendly!'

'Not friendly at all!' agreed Mick.

'So we're gonna drink it an' tell you if we like it!' said Pod with a nasty smirk.

With that he unscrewed the lid and raised it to his mouth. Then he stopped and his nose wrinkled as the smell hit him.

'Yuk!!' he spluttered. 'It's sick!' He spun towards

me, glaring. 'So! Trying to play a trick on me, Dickens?'

Luckily for me, he'd let go of my ear. I knew it was no use trying to point out to him that it was he who'd taken the pot from my bag, and I wasn't trying to play any trick on him. I took the chance and ran. I also knew that even if I ran as fast as I'd ever run before, I wouldn't reach home before they caught up with me and bashed me up, so I ran straight back into school. As I'd hoped, they didn't follow me because they knew that teachers and Mr Morton would still be there. Instead, Pod shouted after me, 'We'll get you for this, Dickens! See if we don't!'

By then I had made it to the school buildings and got inside, but the trouble was, my evidence had gone! If I was going to find out what was in the sick the three little kids had vomited, I had to get hold of some more.

I hurried along to Miss Polska's classroom. The door was open and the cleaners were inside,

sweeping up. The place smelt of disinfectant and the floor was clear. Mr Morton had cleaned up the sick.

I hurried off to Mr Morton's room. There was just a chance that the bucket with the vomit in it might not have been emptied yet. I was out of luck. The bucket was in the corner of the room, empty.

My heart sank.

Then I saw the mop standing beside the bucket, and I was sure there were traces of vomit on the end. I examined it closer. Yes, I was right! There were definitely traces of vomit there. All right, it wouldn't be three separate samples, but this was better than nothing.

The problem was the mop was too long for me to sneak home. It was also likely that I'd get seen by one of the cleaners if I carried the long mop out of school. There was only one answer, and that was to take the head of the mop from the handle and take that with me.

This time I slipped on a pair of my own latex gloves to protect against any germs, then I unscrewed the mop head. I found a plastic sack in a cupboard, put the mop head in it, stuffed them into my bag, and left.

CHAPTER 15

Luckily for me, Pod, Jaz and Mick had gone by the time I left the school. But, just in case they were lying in wait for me, every time I came to a corner on my way home, I peered round it first to make sure the coast was clear.

With all of this, it was well past my usual time for getting home. Mum was waiting for me, and she didn't look pleased.

'Your sister's still in a foul mood,' she said.

'Well, that's not my fault,' I said.

'And you're late.'

'I got held up at school.'

Mum looked past me. 'Where's Kevin?' she asked.

I did my best to look innocent. 'Isn't he here?' I asked.

Mum looked at me, shocked. 'You mean you've lost him?!' she demanded.

'Well … no,' I began. 'I thought he was on his way home, and I hurried after him, but he gave me the slip …'

She wasn't listening to me. She just stared at me, horrified. 'You've *lost* him!' she repeated, only now she said it a different way, like I'd committed some terrible crime.

'I didn't actually *lose* him …' I started to say.

Mum looked at me grimly, and then she pointed an accusing finger towards the door.

'Get out there and find him!' she ordered sternly.

I looked back at her, helplessly. 'Where?' I asked. 'He could be anywhere!'

'Oh God!' she groaned. 'I'll have to call the police! He could be out there wandering, lost and helpless!'

Not Kevin, I thought. He'll be out there spying on people and getting them arrested.

'I'll find him,' I promised her. 'Trust me.'

'I did trust you, and this is what happened!'

she snapped angrily.

I sped out of the house before she could carry on telling me what a dreadful boy I was. Fred was standing by his kennel on his chain. He wagged his tail when he saw me.

'Sorry, Fred,' I said. 'I can't take you with me this time. Whatever Kevin's up to, it's bound to be trouble. You're safest back here. But I'll take you for a walk when I get back.'

I left the house, wondering where Kevin could be. Then it struck me that, if he was still up to his detecting game, he might be at Banger's, spying. Or he could be involved in something with Anwar. I remembered Kevin and Anwar talking in the school playground, all very conspiratorial. And Anwar looking very shifty when we asked him what he and Kevin had been talking about. 'Top Secret,' he'd said. So maybe Kevin was doing something Top Secret with Anwar.

Whichever it was, whether it was spying on Banger Bates or hanging around doing something

Top Secret with Kevin, my guess was I'd find Kevin on the Grove Farm Estate.

CHAPTER 16

I was right. In fact, I was doubly right: as I neared Banger's house I saw Kevin with Anwar and two other little kids. They were hiding behind a low brick wall. Anwar had a pair of binoculars and was training them on Banger's house, while Kevin was talking to the two other little kids, who were listening and nodding. They all looked very serious. I imagined Kevin was telling the little kids they were on a stake-out.

I walked up to them, and as I got near I demanded, 'Kevin! What are you doing?'

I had hardly got the words out before Kevin had leapt at me and pulled me down to the ground.

'Quick! Hide!' he said urgently.

'Get off!' I snapped, pushing him off me and

getting back to my feet.

'We're spying!' said Anwar.

'And not doing a very good job of it!' I told him crossly. 'I could see you from miles away.'

'They're still learning observation techniques,' explained Kevin.

'They shouldn't be here at all!' I exploded. I turned on Anwar. 'Does Suki know what you're up to, Anwar?'

'I told her I was playing with my friends,' he said.

I turned on Kevin. 'You're teaching him to lie!' I said accusingly.

'He's not lying,' said Kevin. 'He is playing with his friends. This is Benji and this is Mark. They're in his class at school.'

'They're spying!'

'Playing at spying,' corrected Kevin. Suddenly he stiffened. 'Look out!' he whispered urgently. 'He's coming!'

'Who's coming?' I demanded.

I realised I was talking to myself. Kevin, Anwar

and the other two had flung themselves down behind the low wall so they were out of sight. Kevin punched me in the knee and I fell over, and joined them on the ground behind the wall.

'Shh!!' said Kevin. 'Watch!'

I looked in the same direction the four would-be spies were looking. Banger was walking along the street, eating chips from a paper bag. And next to him, walking along and jabbering away, looking up at him admiringly, was Shelly! I could hear her talking from this distance.

'I admire a boy with muscles,' she said. 'Most of the boys at our school just work and study. They're so boring!'

'Yeah,' said Banger, 'all that school stuff is boring.' And he stuffed a handful of chips into his mouth.

'I haven't got a boyfriend at the moment,' said Shelly, 'but if I had he'd be about your height. And with muscles like yours. And he'd eat food like you do.'

'Chips,' said Banger. 'And burgers and kebabs.
Good food.'

Banger finished the last of the chips and
scrunched up the chip paper and threw it down on

the ground. Immediately, the little kid nearest to me, Benji, leapt up out of hiding and shouted at him, 'Littering is a crime!'

FACTOID:
Littering

Litter is a health hazard as well as making a place look bad. Some litter takes a long time to break down: aluminium cans can last between 200 and 400 years, polystyrene for 90 years, chewing gum up to 25 years; and plastic shopping bags up to 30 years.

I groaned. The little kids had obviously been lectured at by Kevin about how crime was everywhere, and Benji had taken it too much to heart.

I managed to peer through a gap in the wall and saw Banger turn towards Benji and scowl.

'Who you talking to?' he demanded.

Shelly let out a gasp and put her hands to her

mouth. 'You're so macho, Edward!' she sighed.

Banger ignored her, just kept his glare on the little kid, who was now standing there opening and closing his mouth like a goldfish. Benji had obviously realised that his instinctive reaction to Banger's littering crime had put him right in the firing line for a punch in the nose.

'Come here, you little squirt!' snarled Banger.

That did it. Benji decided to run away as fast as he could. The only trouble was, he had the worst sense of direction of any kid I'd ever seen, and he ran straight into Banger, who grabbed Benji with one of his powerful hands and held him up off the ground.

'You were hiding behind that wall spying on me!' Banger snapped accusingly and menacingly.

'Er …' gurgled Benji.

'Why?' demanded Banger, his tone of voice even more aggressive.

'We … we … we're watching you to get evidence that you're a cheat about being sick!'

stammered Benji.

Banger glared at him. 'Who says I'm a cheat?' he demanded aggressively.

'Dave Dickens,' said the kid.

I felt a sense of doom closing in on me as I heard these words, which got worse as I heard Benji utter the further words, 'He's over there.'

I didn't need to look over the wall to guess that Benji was pointing to where we were hiding, but I did. I was right. Banger and Benji had both turned towards the low wall where we were, the little kid pointing his finger right at me. I heard a sort of explosion of anger from Banger's mouth.

'Run!' yelled Kevin.

The next second, he, Anwar and the other little kid, Mark, went running off. I was just about to run after them, but I tripped and fell over the low wall. I looked up and saw Banger throw Benji to one side and come stomping towards me. Behind him, Shelly gave a squeal of horror.

'That's Krystal's brother!' she chirruped.

'Leave him to me!' snarled Banger.

I didn't wait to give him the opportunity. I picked myself up off the ground and set off at speed, but I wasn't fast enough. Banger had a surprising turn of speed for someone who was so big and seemed to lumber so slowly everywhere. He grabbed me with one of his enormous hands, catching hold of my jacket and stopping me in my tracks. I struggled to get away, but he hauled me nearer, and now he switched his grip to my throat, wrapping his massive fingers around my neck and lifting me off the ground, just like he'd done with Benji. Benji, I noticed, had taken the opportunity to make a run for it.

Banger thrust his face close to mine.

'I know what you're up to, Dickens,' he snarled. 'I'm warning you. You stay out of my business or I'll bash you up so hard they'll have to find the bits of you to stick 'em back together again. And just to show you I'm not joking …'

With that, Banger pulled his enormous fist

back. I struggled to get out of his grip, but I knew I was doomed. I was going to get pounded into little bits!

CHAPTER 17

'What's going on, Edward?'

I looked round. Banger Bates's gran was standing there, looking at us in surprise. Immediately Banger let me go.

'Hello, Gran,' he said. Then he patted me on the head. 'Me and Dickens were just playing … er … cops and robbers.'

Banger's gran looked at me, and then her face lit up when she saw it was me and she gave me a big smile. 'Dave Dickens!' she said. 'How's my lovely Fred keeping?' Then she gave a twinkly smile, winked and said, 'I mean, *your* Fred.'

'He's very well, thank you, Mrs Bates,' I said.

Fred used to belong to Banger's gran, but looking after him got a bit much for her, so she asked me if

I'd like to take him in, especially once I'd stopped him dropping those really powerful farts he used to let off.

'You must bring him round to see me next time you're in this area,' she said.

'I will,' I promised.

And I would, because Banger's gran is a really nice old lady. It always puzzles me about relatives: how you can have someone really nice in the same family as someone who's the worst person on the planet. Like me and my terrifying sister Krystal. And bully Banger Bates and his really nice gran.

'Well, I must go,' I told her. 'It's time to get Fred his dinner.'

I was thinking that it would be best for me to get going before Banger's gran disappeared and Banger started on me again. But, luckily, his gran was going into the Bates' house. She held out a dish covered in silver foil towards Banger.

'Carry this indoors for me, Edward,' she said. 'It's a shepherd's pie I've cooked for you and your dad.'

Banger had no choice but to take the plate from her, and I took the opportunity to run off. I saw Banger give me a nasty look as I did. I also noticed that Shelly had disappeared from the scene.

As I skidded round the corner, I ran straight into Kevin.

'Brilliant, Dave!' said Kevin. 'Running off like that to draw Banger away so we could all escape! Brilliant! It was just like *CSI* ...'

'It was nothing like *CSI*!' I exploded. 'I ran away to get away from him! What were you and that crowd of little kids up to?'

'They're my Irregulars.'

I looked at him, baffled. 'Irregular what?' I asked.

'Like in Sherlock Holmes,' said Kevin. 'He has this gang of kids called the Baker Street Irregulars and they sneak around doing detective work for him. It's clever because no one suspects them of being detectives because they're just ordinary kids. They can go places adults can't.'

I stared at him. 'You're mad!' I said. 'Those little

kids are only six. They're tiny!'

'Which is why Banger and his dad would never know they were spying on them to get evidence that they're running a scam!'

'They know now!' I exploded. 'That little kid told Banger what you were up to! And he said it was because of me!'

Kevin shrugged.

'Yes, well, Benji's only little, and sooner or later everyone cracks under torture. Even James Bond ...'

I groaned. 'You are not James Bond!'

'No, but doesn't he have some fantastic gadgets?' said Kevin, his eyes shining. 'I wish I had gadgets like that. Then I'd be a brilliant detective!'

I managed to get Kevin back home without anything else bad happening to us, but only by keeping a tight grip on his coat so he couldn't run off and start detecting and upsetting people.

Mum was waiting for us as we got home, and she immediately started in on me again for letting Kevin be out 'unprotected'. Kevin didn't try and come up with any excuses this time to save me, he just mumbled, 'Sorry, Aunt Sandra,' and then hurried upstairs to my room.

I was about to go after him, but Mum grabbed me before I could reach the stairs so she could continue with her lecture. It was all about 'responsibility', and looking after those 'younger and more vulnerable than yourself'. I tried to point out that Kevin was actually only about nine months younger than me, but it didn't work. Mum then started on the theme that Kevin was a stranger in this area and there were lots of dangers lying in wait for him. In the end it was simpler for me to just shut up and drop my head in a guilty way and say I was sorry, and it wouldn't happen again.

I was just about to escape from her, when the door opened and Dad came in from work.

'Hello!' he said cheerfully. Then he saw Mum's grim expression and asked, 'What's up?'

'It's Dave,' said Mum. 'He left Kevin to wander the streets on his own.'

'No!' said Dad, shocked.

'I'm going up to my room,' I said.

I nearly made it to the stairs, but, once again, Mum grabbed me and pulled me back.

'Oh no, you don't get off that lightly,' she said. 'Not after what you've done. It's only fair that your Dad knows what's happened, and you can stay here and listen while I tell him.'

And so, once again, I was forced to stand there like the Worst Criminal Ever and listen to Mum tell Dad about how I'd left Kevin alone to wander the streets and be exposed to all the dangers of our town. Honestly, to hear Mum talk you'd have thought we were living in some really dangerous place in South America.

Finally she stopped for breath. Dad turned and looked at me and gave a sad sigh. 'I hope you've learnt your lesson, Dave,' he said in a serious tone of voice.

'I have,' I assured him.

'Good,' he said. 'From now on, you have to keep

an eye on Kevin while he's with us.'

'I will,' I promised him.

And then I turned and headed for the stairs.

'Oh, by the way,' said Dad, 'did you get your box?'

I turned and looked at him, puzzled. 'What box?'

'The one your friend came round for this morning.'

I was still puzzled. 'Which friend?'

'That big boy in your class. Edward Bates.'

I stared at him, and a feeling of dread clutched at my heart. 'Banger Bates?' I whispered hoarsely, barely able to speak.

'It's not nice to call someone Banger,' said Dad. 'I'm sure he prefers to be called by his proper name. Anyway, he came round this morning and said you'd sent him because you'd left your box at home and there was something you needed urgently at school today. He said it was at the bottom of your wardrobe, so I went up and got it, and there it was.' He smiled. 'It was lucky I was home, really. I was supposed to be out pricing up a new bathroom at Heather Avenue, but Mrs Pringle had to go out.'

I'd stopped listening to him. All I could think of was the fact that my evidence had gone! The box with the vomit in it! Banger had stolen it! But how had he known where it was?

I struggled to remember the morning at school, when we were lining up waiting to go in. That was the only time I'd said where I'd hidden the bag of vomit. Banger must have been hanging around, near the class line, and overheard me telling Paul and Suki. That was why he'd been late for school! He must have come rushing round to our house as soon as he heard me say where the sample of his vomit was!

'Anyway, everything turned out all right,' said Dad cheerfully. 'You got it, and that's the main thing. What was in the box, anyway?'

'A bag with vomit in it,' I said gloomily.

Mum scowled. 'There's no need to be rude,' she said.

'Yes,' added Dad, looking put out. 'You ought to learn some manners and be polite like that Edward Bates.' He looked thoughtful. 'It has to be said that me and your mum used to think he was a bit of a bad lot. But meeting him again today, with him being so polite and helpful – going out of his way to do an errand for you – it just shows that people can change!'

There was nothing I could say to that. My heart felt so heavy. All I could do was give a big sigh and go up to my room.

Even there, there was no escape from my misery. Kevin was in my room.

CHAPTER 18

What was worse, he was on my laptop.

'What are you doing?!' I demanded, annoyed.

'Research,' said Kevin cheerfully. 'This whole business of Banger and the vomit scam is like this episode of this detective show I saw. It's that detective doctor, you know …'

'No I don't know!' I exploded. 'You shouldn't be using my computer without asking.'

'OK,' said Kevin. 'Can I use your computer?'

'No,' I said firmly.

Kevin looked at me, a pained expression on his face.

'Huh!' he said. 'That's all the thanks I get for helping you.'

I stared at him, shocked at his outrageous cheek.

'*Helping* me?' I echoed, adding a sarcastic snort to make my point.

Kevin looked concerned. 'It sounds like your nose is blocked,' he said. 'Banger Bates might have damaged your nose when he hit you.'

'My nose is not blocked!' I snapped at him. 'That was a sarcastic snort!'

'Why?' asked Kevin, now looking puzzled.

I ticked the reasons off on my fingers. 'One, you got me in trouble with my mum and dad by sneaking off on your own. B, you got me in dangerous trouble with Banger Bates …'

'Why have you switched from "One" to "b"?' asked Kevin. 'It should be one then two, or a then b …'

'Shut up! I have enough of a problem with you making my life a misery without you making it worse by all this talk about a and b …'

'Ah, but I know how to get Banger to confess!' said Kevin, smirking. 'We entrap him!'

I groaned. Kevin just wasn't taking this in! 'We are not going to entrap him, or anyone else,' I told him firmly. 'Banger Bates is dangerous. He's also clever.'

Kevin looked puzzled at that one. 'You told me

that he's stupid,' he said.

'Yes, he is,' I admitted. 'But he was clever enough to take the evidence from my wardrobe this morning.'

Kevin's mouth dropped open, and then he gave a yelp of delight. 'Great!' he said. 'He'll have left fingerprints! We can have him arrested for burglary!'

FACTOID:
Fingerprints
Fingerprints weren't used as part of crime investigation until the late part of the 19th century.

'No we can't, because my dad gave him the box.' Briefly, I told him what had happened.

Kevin sighed and shook his head. 'Adults can be so stupid,' he said. 'It's just like in this episode of *Poirot* ...'

Luckily, before he could start telling me the

whole story of this TV episode, Mum called up from downstairs to tell us that tea was ready.

It was pretty quiet at tea, mainly because Krystal was still up in her room sulking about Shelly and because Mum and Dad kept giving me pointed looks, as if they were waiting for me to take Kevin out into the garden and bury him, or something equally horrible. We had the local TV news on as we ate, and once again there was an item about our school. Once again it was about vomit, and this time Banger Bates's dad stood looking into the camera with Banger and the three little kids who'd been sick in Anwar's class standing beside him.

'There is some kind of epidemic at that school,' intoned Banger's dad. 'I demand a public enquiry.' And then, in case he hadn't made the point strongly enough last time, he added firmly, 'And compensation for those who have suffered. Like these poor children here.'

And the camera then went on to Banger and the three little kids from Anwar's class, who all did their best to look like poor workhouse orphans from *Oliver Twist*.

Then the camera switched to the reporter, who said, 'We have spoken to the school and we understand that the school kitchen will be closed tomorrow while an inspection is carried out. Parents are being advised to send their children to school with a packed lunch.'

On cue, the phone rang, and Mum went to answer it. We heard her say, 'Yes, Mrs Nelson. We've just seen that on the news. No, no problem. I'll send both Dave and Kevin in with something for them to eat at lunch.'

I imagined how Paul must be feeling right at that moment, seeing this on TV. He would be really worried about his mum's job. And, what was worse, we all knew it was a fake, a scam by Banger and his dad; but the evidence I'd collected to prove that had been stolen.

There had to be some way to defeat the Bateses! We had to stop it before it got out of hand and Paul's mum lost her job. I had to see Paul and Suki and put our brains together and come up with an answer.

After tea, I told my mum that I was taking Fred for a walk.

'Good idea,' she said. 'You can take Kevin with you.'

I'd thought she might say this, so I had my answer ready. 'I'd love to,' I said, 'but sometimes Kevin runs off. That's OK when it's just me and him, but if Fred is loose in the park I won't be able to get him back quick enough to go after Kevin, and Kevin might end up loose and wandering around the streets …'

Mum glared suspiciously at me, and I'd wondered if I'd gone a bit too far in using her own words. But I could see her struggling with a decision. She knew what Kevin was like, and she knew what I said about Fred running around the park was also true.

'Very well,' she said. 'But don't get into trouble!'

'I won't,' I promised her.

With that, I put Fred on his lead and hurried off before Mum could change her mind.

CHAPTER 19

I made straight for Paul's house. It took longer than it usually did to get there because I had to go round loads of different streets to make sure I didn't go past Banger's house in case he saw me. At the same time I was also on the look-out for Banger's gang, because if they spotted me I'd be in dead trouble, even though I had Fred with me as protection.

When I got to Paul's, he was sitting on his front step looking miserable, but he brightened up when he saw me.

'When are we going to produce that evidence and save my mum?' he asked eagerly. 'That sick of Banger's.'

'Er ... actually there's a problem there,' I said.

Paul looked puzzled.

'What sort of problem?' he asked.

I looked around warily, expecting Banger to appear at any moment and grab me.

'Let's go to the park,' I said. 'We'll be safer there. There's less chance of Banger and his gang finding us.'

'What sort of problem?' he repeated, more urgently this time.

'Banger stole the evidence,' I told him gloomily.

Paul looked shocked. 'What!' he said, stunned. 'How?'

'I'll tell you as we go to the park,' I said.

Paul stared at me, still shocked, then he said, 'We ought to bring Suki in. She's clever. We could do with her brain.'

'You go and get her,' I told him. 'It's not safe for me to go too near Banger's house. I'll see you at the park.'

'OK,' said Paul. 'But don't go anywhere else until we've talked. My mum's really worried.'

I let Paul go to find Suki, while I took Fred to the park to wait for them.

There were the usual people at the park: a few joggers running around with headphones on and bottles of water in their hands, mums and dads with little kids in pushchairs, and people with dogs, following their dogs around with pooper scoopers and plastic bags. I let Fred off the lead and he ran off happily to meet up with some of his doggy friends. Fred has got a small gang of dogs he runs around with when we go to the park: there's a little white terrier with very short legs that runs as fast as it can but can't keep up with the other dogs, a tall and thin reddy-brownish dog that can run faster than any of the others, a big fat dog that can't run at all, and Fred. What usually happens is that they all run around chasing each other and then running away again, and then chasing each other again, just like little kids in the playground at school. I think it's good for Fred because it means he gets lots of exercise which helps his digestive system and stops his farts being so lethal, and he knows he's got friends apart from me.

FACTOID:
Breeds of Dogs
There are hundreds and hundreds of different breeds of dogs. Dogs are mainly put into one of five categories: guard dogs (e.g. German shepherd); hunting dogs (e.g. hounds and spaniels); herding dogs (e.g. Border collie); working dogs (e.g. St Bernard; husky); and companion dogs (e.g. Chihuahua).

Today there was only the little white terrier with the short legs at the park, but they were soon running off playing a game which involved dodging in and out of the joggers. It was actually quite interesting to watch because the joggers would be running along very determinedly, and suddenly they'd find a little white terrier under their feet and they'd do all manner of jumping up and down to stop themselves tripping over.

Paul, Suki and Anwar turned up soon after I'd got to the park. Suki let Anwar run off to join in chasing around with Fred and the terrier, while I told Suki and Paul what had happened with Banger going round to my house and getting the sample of sick from my wardrobe.

'It's the end!' groaned Paul. 'My mum will get the blame and she'll get the sack.'

'No she won't,' said Suki. 'Remember, Dave got those other samples of sick from the kids in Anwar's class. They'll do.'

'No they won't,' I said gloomily, and I told them

about Banger's gang taking them off me. 'I got some other samples of the same sick from Mr Morton's mop head, but I don't think it'll be as good. There's no way of proving who vomited up what from the mop head.'

'Then we're sunk!' said Paul miserably.

'Oh no we're not!' said a cheerful voice behind me.

I spun round, shocked. Kevin was standing there!

'What are you doing here?' I demanded.

Kevin winked. 'I used the old "climb down the drainpipe" dodge.' He grinned. 'It's a classic! All the best detectives and spies use it. Don't worry, no one saw me.'

'But … but … why?' I asked, still shocked.

'Because you need me,' said Kevin. 'I am the detective on this case!'

'No you're not!' I snapped at him. 'You are my irritating cousin who keeps getting me in trouble!'

Kevin just grinned. 'Good old Dave!' he said. 'It's great that you can keep your sense of humour.'

Paul and Suki were still staring at Kevin, as stunned as I was by his appearance.

'You climbed down a drainpipe?' asked Paul.

'Yep,' said Kevin. 'But first you have to check that the drainpipe is fixed securely to the wall.'

'And how are you going to get back in?' I demanded. 'Climb up the drainpipe?'

'No,' said Kevin. 'You'll get me back in.'

'How?' I asked.

Kevin shrugged. 'We'll think of something,' he said airily. 'But right now we have to work out how to prove that Banger Bates made those kids in Anwar's class vomit.'

'We don't know for sure that he did,' said Suki.

'Oh yes we do!' said Kevin confidently. 'Anwar!'

His call bought Anwar, plus Fred and the little terrier, running over to us.

'Anwar,' said Kevin, 'tell them about the Bandit Cards.'

'We already know about Bandit Cards,' I told him.

You know how every now and then there's a new craze at school. Well, right now it was Bandit Cards, with all the little kids collecting these cards with pictures of Bandits on them from the *Bandits* TV show.

'Ah, but what you don't know is that Banger bribed those three kids who were sick with them,' said Kevin. 'Tell them, Anwar.'

Anwar nodded. 'I saw Banger giving them cards at lunchtime; so after I asked them, and they told me he'd given them the cards if they could pretend to be sick. He told them how to do it, by sticking their fingers down their throats, and told them that if they did it and actually made themselves sick he'd give them two more Bandit Cards each.'

'Anwar's one of my Irregulars,' said Kevin proudly. 'I'm training him to be a detective.'

Suki swung round to look at me. She looked angry. 'Did you know about this, Dave?' she demanded, obviously upset.

'Not until this afternoon, when I found Anwar

with two of his friends and Kevin keeping watch on Banger.'

'And Dave saved us from getting bashed up by Banger!' Kevin told her proudly.

Suki shook her head, still angry. 'I have enough of a problem keeping Anwar out of trouble as it is,' she said. 'This stuff with Kevin, playing at detectives, is only going to make things worse for me!'

'We're not *playing* at detectives,' Anwar told her. 'We *are* detectives!'

'No you're not,' Suki said to him firmly. Turning to Kevin, she said, 'I don't want you playing with my brother any more. 'Then, to me and Paul, she said, 'I'm sorry, but I'm taking Anwar home. I wondered why he's been such a nuisance at home, following me and my mum and dad and my aunts everywhere. Well, now I know.' And she turned back once again to Kevin. 'Understand? Stay away from Anwar.' With that, she took hold of Anwar's hand and started to head for the park gates, but Anwar began to struggle.

'No!' he yelled. 'Let me go! I want to be a detective!'

'Stop it!' shouted Suki. And her voice sounded so angry it shocked Anwar into silence. To be honest, it shocked me and Paul as well – Suki is usually such a quiet, gentle person.

'I'll see you at school tomorrow,' Suki said to us. Then she turned on Kevin and added her final warning to him, 'Remember what I said, no more playing with Anwar.'

With that, she left.

CHAPTER 20

Kevin shrugged, then smiled brightly at me and Paul.

'So!' he said cheerfully. 'It's just us, the three musketeers!'

FACTOID:
The Three Musketeers
The Three Musketeers was an adventure story written by Alexandre Dumas. The Three Musketeers were Athos, Porthos and Aramis.

'We are not the three musketeers!' I told him firmly. 'It's just me and Paul, and I shall prove that Banger's behind it my way! Scientifically! With evidence!'

'But you haven't got any evidence,' Kevin pointed out. 'Banger stole it.'

'There's the sick on the mop,' I said.

'You said it wouldn't be any use,' said Paul.

'And, because the kids who made themselves sick did eat school dinners, it will have traces of school dinner in the sick,' added Kevin.

I stared at him. He was right!

Paul groaned. 'This is a disaster!' he said. 'My mum's definitely going to lose her job!'

'No!' said Kevin. 'Because we have a plan!'

Paul and I looked at Kevin, puzzled.

'What plan?' I asked.

'The plan to get Banger to confess!'

I let out a hollow laugh. 'And how do you propose we do that?' I demanded. 'We can't frighten him into confessing, we're all too scared of him.'

'So we trick him,' said Kevin.

'How?' asked Paul.

'We get him to boast about what he's done! And we record him boasting about it!'

I gave a sarcastic snort. 'And how do you suggest we do that?' I demanded. 'He's not going to admit that sort of thing to us, is he!'

'No, but he would to that girl who fancies him. His stalker.'

Paul looked at me, bewildered. 'There's a girl who fancies Banger?' he asked.

'Yes,' I said.

'Who on this planet would fancy Banger?' he demanded.

'Shelly,' I told him.

Paul stared at me, bewildered. 'Not your sister Krystal's friend, Shelly?' he asked.

'Yes,' I nodded.

Paul paused to let this sink in. He didn't look convinced. 'The one with the blonde curly hair who goes all twee about things?' he asked, making sure we were talking about the same Shelly.

'Yes,' I nodded.

Paul still looked doubtful. 'I don't believe it,' he said, shaking his head.

'It's true,' I said.

Briefly, Kevin and I told him about Shelly asking Banger for his autograph, and what Krystal had told her friend about Shelly thinking Banger was 'hunky'. Then I told Paul about seeing Shelly with Banger when he nearly bashed me up.

Paul shook his head again. 'Shelly fancying Banger,' he muttered in a tone of astonishment. 'The world's gone mad.'

'The point is, he might admit what he's up to, to her,' Kevin said.

'So what?' demanded Paul. 'She's not likely to tell us what he says to her, even if he does admit it!'

'No, but he might admit it if he *thought* he was talking to her,' continued Kevin. 'But instead he'd be talking to one of us!'

I glared at Kevin. 'If you think I'm putting on a dress and a wig with golden curls and going round his house …' I began.

'No, we text him!' Kevin said. 'Pretending to be

her! Or, even better, we email him and get him to admit it that way! In print!'

FACTOID:
Texting
The first recorded text message was sent in December 1992 by a test engineer to a friend from his personal computer via the Vodafone network. The message said, 'Merry Christmas'.

I stared at Kevin. It was mad! I had never heard anything so stupid! Then Paul spoke.

'That's brilliant!' he said, a tone of awe in his voice.

I looked at him, surprised. 'Brilliant?' I echoed. 'It's stupid! For one thing, how will we get hold of Shelly's phone? We can't use any other phone because he'll recognise the number. Same with sending him an email. He'll see the address it really came from.'

'Details, details,' shrugged Kevin. 'We can work that out.'

'It's brilliant,' repeated Paul. 'Kevin, you are a genius!'

'He's not a genius!' I protested.

Kevin gave a modest grin. 'It's what a true detective does,' he said. Then something behind my shoulder caught his eye, because he said, 'I think you ought to do something about your dog, Dave.'

I turned, and saw that one of the joggers was lying on the grass, and Fred and the little terrier were playing chase around him and over him.

I hurried over and put Fred's lead on him.

'Are you all right?' I asked the jogger.

'I tripped over that little dog,' said the jogger, pushing himself up. 'And then that big dog farted right in my face. I couldn't breathe.'

'Methane,' I apologised. 'It'll wear off.'

FACTOID:
Methane

Methane is a greenhouse gas, which means it is a major contributor to climate change. The earth's crust contains massive amounts of methane, as do mud volcanoes, landfill sites and cattle.

CHAPTER 21

Kevin and I left Paul, and then walked home with Fred. All the way home Kevin kept up a stream of talk about how we could put his scheme into action. I have to say, although I'd said it was a stupid plan, part of me had to admit that it was clever, and I wished I'd thought of it.

The problem was, how were we going to text Banger and make him think the text was coming from Shelly's phone? And how could we get him to text us back, and not Shelly? The only way to do that would be to actually use Shelly's phone, and that would be hard to get hold of.

As we got near home I hesitated, wondering how we were going to sneak Kevin in without Mum and Dad seeing him; but instead Kevin just walked in openly. Mum looked at him and said, 'I thought you were upstairs, Kevin.'

'I was,' said Kevin, 'but I remembered that the roof of Fred's kennel needed fixing, so I popped out to do it and saw Dave coming back.'

'You're a good boy,' said Mum. 'It's a pleasure to have someone so helpful staying with us, isn't it, Dave?'

I was stunned into silence. He'd told a bare-faced lie and got away with it! If I'd tried something like that there would have been all sorts of questions asked. Life is not fair!

I put Fred on his chain and then headed upstairs to my room. I wanted to have a serious talk with Kevin in private about his idea of using Shelly's phone. However, as I got to my room, Krystal's door opened and she shot out like an angry rat and cornered me against the wall. This close up, she looked even more terrifying than usual.

'Shelly texted me to tell me you were spying on her!' she raged. 'You've made me look like an idiot!

She thinks I care about what she does and where she goes because of you!'

'I wasn't spying on her!' I protested. 'I was trying to stop Kevin getting me in trouble.'

'That's typical of you!' snapped back Krystal. 'You mess up my life and you blame it on someone else!' She grabbed me by the hair and pulled me up so I was standing on my tip-toes. I could feel the roots of my hair coming out.

FACTOID:
Hair
People have about 1 million hairs growing on their heads. Human hair grows at the rate of about 1cm a month.

'From now on, stay away from Shelly!' she snarled. 'You have been warned!'

With that, she stormed back into her room and slammed the door. I stood there for a few seconds, blinking my eyes to try and see through the tears of pain that had filled them up. When they finally cleared I found myself staring into Kevin's face.

'Wow!' he said, impressed. 'Krystal's more frightening than she used to be! That hair grip thing she did on you looked really painful.'

'It *was* really painful,' I told him, rubbing my head.

'Why didn't you do kung-fu on her?' he asked. 'That's what James Bond does! You could have twisted round and thrown her over your shoulder, and she'd have fallen downstairs.'

'Then she would have come back up and torn me limb from limb,' I pointed out to him.

Kevin shook his head. 'You ought to learn a martial art,' he told me. 'I'm learning karate.' He held up his fist. 'I can break concrete blocks in half with this.' Then he thought about what he'd just said, and added, 'Well, I will be able to once I've mastered it. At the moment I'm still on lesson one, which is about balancing on one leg.'

I followed him into my room.

'So?' he said. 'How are we going to get hold of Shelly's phone?'

'We can't,' I said. 'For one thing, if I go anywhere near Shelly, Krystal says she'll kill me. And we can hardly take Shelly's phone off her without her noticing it's gone.'

And then it hit me. A stroke of genius! 'Yes we can!' I said.

Kevin looked at me, puzzled. 'Yes we can, what?' he asked.

'Swap Shelly's phone without her noticing.'

'How?'

'Because Krystal's got a phone that's absolutely identical! It's got dreadful pink and yellow swirling patterns all over it, and it's exactly the same make and model. Krystal got the same one as Shelly when they were best friends.'

'Brilliant!' said Kevin delightedly. 'So all we have to do is get Krystal's phone off her and switch it with Shelly's! Then we use Shelly's to text Banger. When we get his reply we forward that to someone else's phone, and the internet, so we've got it in writing. Then we swap Shelly's phone back again!'

When it was put into words like that, it sounded simple. The big problems were:

a) Getting hold of Krystal's phone without her noticing.

b) Hanging on to Krystal's phone long enough to swap it with Shelly's, without Shelly noticing.

c) Swapping Shelly's and Krystal's phones back after we'd got Banger's confession.

d) Putting Krystal's phone back without her being suspicious about what had happened to it.

Frankly, all along the line, a), b), c) and d), there were places where it was quite likely that whoever was handling these phones would be in serious danger of being bashed up, either by Krystal or Banger, or shouted at by Shelly. And so far, it looked as if the person doing this phone business was Yours Truly.

And then I had another stroke of genius! How to get Shelly to hand over her phone without me being in serious danger. Well, maybe just a bit of danger, but I could get out of that providing Mum or Dad were around. And the answer was ... dog poo!

CHAPTER 22

'What?' asked Kevin, a look of bewilderment on his face.

'Dog poo,' I said again. 'It's the answer!'

'What was the question?' he asked, still looking puzzled. 'What comes out of a dog's bum?'

'No,' I said. I was just about to explain my brilliant idea to him when Mum called up the stairs, 'Dave! It's the phone for you!'

Immediately I was suspicious. Who would be calling me? Maybe it was Banger Bates, or one of his gang, phoning to threaten me.

'Dave!' called Mum again. 'It's Suki for you!'

Straight away I relaxed and hurried down to take the phone.

'Hello,' I said.

'I'm sorry I spoke the way I did earlier, Dave,' she said. 'I wasn't having a go at you. It was just that I found out why Anwar had been behaving the way he has lately.'

'But Anwar's always like that,' I pointed out. 'He's like a human mini-destruction machine.'

'Yes, but lately he's been worse,' said Suki. 'He's been creeping around, watching everyone. My aunt went to the toilet and found him hiding in the shower. And when my dad went to bed for an afternoon snooze, Anwar was hiding under it recording him snoring. He's been terrible! And when I found out he was doing it because of your cousin, Kevin …'

'Now you know what I have to put up with,' I said.

'Yes,' she said. 'So, I'm sorry. But I still want to help prove that it's Banger who's behind these kids being sick, and not Paul's mum's school dinners. So, if there's anything I can do …'

'Yes, there is,' I said. I looked around, checking on whether Mum or Dad was listening. Or even

Krystal. Even though I couldn't see them, it didn't mean they weren't there. Or maybe I'd been spending too much time with Kevin and was starting to imagine I was being watched.

'I'll see you at school tomorrow and tell you about the plan,' I said.

'Right,' she said.

I hung up, and immediately Kevin popped up.

'We have a plan?' he asked, eagerly.

See! I knew someone had been listening to my phone conversation. I might have known it would be Kevin.

'I'll tell you about it upstairs,' I said.

When we were back in my room, I explained the 'dog poo' business.

'Krystal hates anything she thinks of as disgusting,' I said. 'Snot, vomit, pee and especially poo.'

'Lots of people are like that,' agreed Kevin.

'So, if Krystal thought that Fred had swallowed her phone and then pooed it out, she'd never want to use it again.'

FACTOID:
Bodily Excretions
If we did not get rid of our body waste
through our poo, pee, sweat, farts, vomit
and snot, we would die.

Kevin looked at me, and for the first time I actually saw a look of awe on his face. 'That's brilliant!' he said.

'Yes, it is,' I agreed. Because it was. 'Now, to do that, there are two problems to overcome. One, getting hold of Krystal's phone. And, two, when she gets mad and says she needs another phone to replace it, we have to have another one ready so we can switch the SIM cards over. Then she'll be happy.'

'I've got another phone!' cried Kevin.

'I know you have,' I said. 'Your mum's. The one you used to call 999.'

'So, we'll use that one,' said Kevin.

'But that doesn't solve the other problem,' I pointed out to him. 'Getting hold of Krystal's phone in the first place. Once I've got it, I can take it outside and say I found it in a lump of Fred's poo, so she'll think it went right through him – but if Krystal catches me stealing her phone ...'

'I can do it!' offered Kevin.

'Are you sure?' I asked him. 'Remember, Krystal is very dangerous. If she catches you ...'

'She won't,' said Kevin confidently, 'because that's what my detective training is all about!' He winked. 'Leave it to me, Dave. I'll put our plan into action right after tea!'

I don't know how Kevin did it, and I didn't ask him, because he'd have gone into some long detailed and boring explanation of how he was a super-spy. The end product was that, soon after tea, Kevin sidled up to me and slipped something into my hand.

'Here,' he whispered, out of the side of his mouth.

It was Krystal's phone.

It was followed a few seconds later by an ear-splitting screech from Krystal upstairs. 'Someone's taken my phone!'

'There's no need to shout, Krystal,' said my mum.

Krystal came stomping downstairs. 'Someone's been in my room and taken my phone!' she thundered. And, of course, she turned on me. 'I bet it was you!'

'No it wasn't!' I said, and I could say that without turning red or looking guilty, because I hadn't. Then I did my 'acting' bit. 'Actually, I thought I saw Fred licking something that looked like your phone. You must have dropped it near his kennel.'

Krystal stared at me, shocked. 'That dog licking my phone!' she echoed, a look of serious distaste on her face.

'I'll go out and see,' I said, and I rushed out to Fred's kennel before anyone could say anything else. Then, I hurried back in, holding Krystal's phone.

'I was right,' I said. 'The trouble is it looks like he might have swallowed it and pooed it out …'

I didn't need to say any more. Krystal let out a screech that must have deafened the whole population living within a fifty-mile radius. When the shockwaves had stopped and we'd all recovered our hearing again, Mum tried to restore calm. In actual fact, if Krystal had thought about it properly she'd have worked out that Fred couldn't have possibly eaten her phone and then pooed it out so soon, because it takes about eight hours for food to work its way through your digestive system,

from mouth to bum. But Krystal wasn't thinking properly; the very thought of Fred even *licking* her phone had grossed her out completely.

'It wasn't Fred's fault,' Mum told Krystal. 'He's just a dog ...'

'And he's pooed my phone!' raged Krystal.

'No he hasn't!' said Mum firmly. 'It takes a long time for anything to get through the digestive system.' As she said this, my heart sank. Mum had blown my scheme! But then she added, 'I expect all he's done is lick it ...'

'He's licked it!' howled Krystal. 'Yuk!! I can never touch that again!' Then she stopped as a horrid thought hit her. 'What am I going to do for a phone?'

The reason for her shock at this is because my sister, like all the other girls at her school, can't seem to live without having her mobile phone with her and texting all her other friends all the time. Even when they're in the same room as each other, they still seem to text each other, even though it would be easier to just talk to one another.

'I've got a spare phone,' piped up Kevin. 'It's my Mum's. You can borrow that until you get another one.'

'But my SIM card's in the one that dog licked,' protested Krystal.

'I'll change the SIM cards over,' offered Kevin.

'Without getting dog dribble on it?' challenged Krystal.

'No problem,' Kevin assured her.

'There,' said Mum, smiling. 'All sorted.'

Krystal still didn't look entirely convinced, but at least she'd have a phone with all her numbers on it. And she cheered up a bit when she saw the mobile that Kevin produced for her. Because it was Aunt Brenda's, it was quite a good-looking phone, so she wouldn't look bad at school when she took it out.

Kevin swapped over the SIM cards, then I took Krystal's phone out to the cold tap in the garden and pretended to clean Fred's saliva off.

'Part one of the Master Plan!' whispered Kevin delightedly, and he gave me a wink. 'We are the dynamic duo, Dave!'

CHAPTER 23

Next morning, Kevin and I arrived at school with our packed lunches. Paul, Suki and Anwar were already there. Paul looked upset.

'My mum's really worried,' he said. 'Because the kitchen's closed today, she and the other cooks have been told to stay at home. She's sure they're going to sack her.' He looked at me, appealing. 'The sooner we can put the plan into operation, the better.'

'What plan?' asked Suki.

Quickly, we filled her in with what we intended to do. I pulled out Krystal's phone and showed it to them.

'The big thing now is swapping this phone with Shelly's so when we send the text, Banger knows it's from Shelly's number. The problem is, if I go anywhere near Shelly she'll tell Krystal, and Krystal will kill me.'

Paul and I looked at Suki hopefully.

Suki sighed. 'OK,' she said. 'I'll see if I can do it. The trouble is, I don't know her enough to talk to. She's sure to get suspicious if I start asking to look at her phone.'

My heart sank. What Suki said was right. Paul looked gloomier than ever. He knew that Suki was right, too.

'We're never going to get Shelly's phone off her,' he said miserably.

'Yes we are!' said Kevin perkily. 'I can do it!'

We all looked at him, surprised.

'How?' I asked.

Kevin grinned. 'Better you don't know,' he said. And he gave one of his cheerful annoying winks again. 'Trade secrets of the detective business!' He held out his hand, and I gave him Krystal's phone.

'I'll get hold of it straight after school,' he said. Then he frowned. 'The one thing I'm not sure I can do is get Banger's reply on to email.'

'I can do that!' said Paul. He took out his own mobile. 'I've been practising with all the things this phone does!'

FACTOID:
Mobile Phone Technology
The first call to be made from a portable hand-held mobile phone was made on 3 April 1973 by the inventor of that phone, Martin Cooper. He made the call to his rival, Dr Joel Engel, who was working to build a mobile phone at Bell Laboratories.

'Great!' said Kevin. 'So, once I've got hold of Shelly's phone I'll come round to your house with it.'

'We'll come round to Paul's house,' I said firmly. 'After the way I got told off for letting you go out alone, I'm staying with you.'

'Excellent!' beamed Kevin. 'You can help me when I get the phone off Shelly!'

I hesitated. 'I've already said, if I go near Shelly, Krystal will kill me,' I reminded him.

'You don't need to,' said Kevin. 'You'll just be there ready to help my get-away, in case there's trouble.'

I looked at him suspiciously. 'Why should there be trouble?' I asked, worried.

Kevin shrugged. 'Who knows?' he said airily. 'When you're on a case, anything can happen.'

Just then the bell went, and it was time for us to get into our class lines. Me, Suki and Paul were heading towards ours, when Mrs Nelson appeared.

'Dave,' she said, 'I want a word with you. In my office. Now. Come with me.'

The way she said it, and the way she looked, I knew this meant trouble. But why? As far as I knew I hadn't done anything wrong. All right, I'd taken the mop head off the mop the night before, but there'd been no one around to see me take it. The cleaners had been in the different classrooms. Why was I in trouble?

Suki and Paul looked at me, sympathetic expressions on their faces as I followed Mrs Nelson into the school. We passed Miss Moore as she was coming out to collect our class.

'I need to have a word with Dave, Miss Moore,' said Mrs Nelson. 'I'll send him along to class afterwards.'

'Right, Mrs Nelson,' said Miss Moore, but I could tell from the puzzled look on her face that she didn't know what it was about either.

We reached Mrs Nelson's office. Mrs Nelson pointed for me to go in.

'Stand there,' she said, indicating a spot in front of her desk. Whatever this was about, her manner was definitely anti-Dave. I began to get seriously worried.

She turned her laptop so that the screen was facing me, then she walked to a small black box on a table.

'It may interest you to know that the school's insurance company insisted that we install closed-circuit TV,' she said. 'Mr Morton switched it on yesterday for the first time.'

She pressed a switch on the black box, and a sequence of pictures appeared on the screen. The first was of me going into Mr Morton's room. Then a picture appeared of me taking Mr Morton's mop and unscrewing the mop head. The last picture was of me walking away.

Mrs Nelson pressed the switch and the picture of me going off carrying the mop head froze. She turned to look at me, her lips pressed together in a hard thin line.

'Well?' she demanded.

I wanted the floor to open up and swallow me.

'Mr Morton is very proud of keeping his equipment safe,' she said. 'This school has a very good record for security. We do not have thefts and burglaries. Or, at least, we didn't until yesterday.' She pointed at the frozen image of me on the screen. 'We have a thief in this school. And his name is Dave Dickens!'

CHAPTER 24

'I'm not a thief!' I burst out, upset. 'I was doing it to save the school! And Paul's mum's job!'

Mrs Nelson looked at me, a baffled expression on her face. 'What?' she said.

'This stuff about the kids being sick,' I said. 'It's not the school dinners. It's Banger Bates!'

Mrs Nelson looked as if she was about to scoff, but then she stopped herself. She looked at me, curious. 'Go on,' she said.

And then I let it all come out. About how Banger hadn't eaten a school dinner the day he was sick, and how he'd bribed the little kids in Miss Walcott's class with Bandit Cards to make themselves sick.

'I was just trying to get samples of the sick from the mop head to see what was in it.'

Mrs Nelson stood looking at me thoughtfully. Finally, she said, 'Are you making this up, Dave, just because you were caught on camera stealing a mop head?'

'No!' I told her. 'It's true! The problem is I can't prove it! Banger took the sample of sick I scraped up. And the little kids in Miss Walcott's class will be too scared of Banger to tell you about their deal with him.'

'His name is Edward,' Mrs Nelson corrected me primly. She walked around her office a bit, still looking thoughtful. Finally, she said, 'You realise it is a very bad thing to make unsubstantiated accusations against someone.'

'They're not unsubstantiated!' I protested. 'I know he did it!'

She shook her head. 'Without proof, they're unsubstantiated,' she said. 'And if you were foolish enough to repeat what you've said to me outside this room, Edward Bates and his family could sue you for slander.' She gave a sigh and sat down in her chair. 'This is all very unfortunate, and I do believe you mean well, Dave. I've always found you to be an honest boy. But this is dangerous ground you are treading on. Unfounded accusations. The threats of legal action. We already have one such action being considered ...'

'It's a scam!' I told her, now feeling much bolder.

Mrs Nelson shook her head. 'There is no proof,' she said. She thought things over a bit more in silence, then she said, 'I will forget the business of the mop head. Providing you return it to me tomorrow.'

'I will,' I promised her.

'As for the other matter, the health authorities are investigating. They will be checking out the school kitchen today.'

'They won't find anything!' I insisted.

'They may not,' agreed Mrs Nelson. 'But right now, the school is under very close scrutiny. Saying anything in public about what you think Edward Bates may or may not be up to, will not help that situation. Is that clear?'

FACTOID:
Food Poisoning

Food poisoning is mostly caused by bacteria contaminating food as a result of poor kitchen hygiene or bad food storage. Proper kitchen hygiene and regular hand-washing is the best way to stop this problem.

'But …' I began.

'Is that clear?' she repeated, her tone very firm this time. To make sure I understood she fixed me with that glare of hers that used to terrify me when I was in the little kids' classes. 'You will make no mention of your allegations against Edward Bates, or anyone else. You have no evidence to back them up. You will only make things worse for this school.'

'But Paul's mum's job …' I protested.

'There will be no further discussion on this issue,' said Mrs Nelson. She stood up. 'Return to your class.'

When I got back to class we were doing silent

reading as part of our literacy hour, so I didn't get the chance to tell Paul and Suki about Mrs Nelson until breaktime. Paul looked even gloomier as I told them about the conversation I'd had with her.

'It sounds like she's going to let my mum take the blame,' he complained.

'She says there isn't any proof that Banger's behind it,' I said.

'Well, there soon will be!' said Kevin.

I jumped. I hadn't even noticed him arriving by our group.

'I wish you wouldn't sneak up on people like that!' I complained.

'It's what we detectives do,' said Kevin. And he smiled. 'Trust me, when this is over, you'll be grateful for it.'

The rest of the day at school was a misery for me. All I could think of was that I was going to be around Kevin when he swapped Krystal's mobile phone with Shelly's, and I just knew that something was bound to go wrong. And when it did, I was going to be the one in trouble. And from two of the scariest people I knew: Krystal and Banger.

Krystal might not be too much of a problem, providing I was able to make sure that whenever Krystal and I were in the same room that Mum or Dad were also around to protect me. The real problem, as I saw it, was Banger.

Banger knew that I suspected him. He also knew I was trying to get evidence to prove he was behind the outbreak of kids at school being sick. He had warned me before of what he would do to me if I carried on investigating and trying to get evidence. Banger grabbed hold of me at lunchtime and warned me again. 'If I find out you've been spying on me, or doing something to prove it was me who made those kids sick, I will chop your body into bits and stuff it into a meat grinder. And don't think I won't. My uncle works at a butcher's.'

In short, if Banger found out that I was using Kevin to get that evidence, I was dead. I'd possibly end up being eaten one tea-time by Mum and

Dad and Krystal as sausages.

When school ended, Paul whispered to me, 'Good luck, Dave! I'll be waiting at home.'

And I'll possibly be hanging on a hook at a butcher's, I thought gloomily. I did think about backing out, but it had gone too far. Someone famous once said, 'All it needs for evil to triumph is for good men to do nothing.' I can't remember who said it, but I remember Miss Moore telling us that's what he said. And it's true. No matter how small we are, it's our duty to stand up and say 'No' to evil people, even if they can bash you up. If enough good people say 'No', then evil can stop. And at this moment there were three of us good people willing to stand up and say 'No', even if we were very scared about doing it. Me, Paul and Suki. I didn't count Kevin as one of the 'good people' because he'd got his mum's boyfriend arrested by the Turkish police, which was a rotten thing to do in my book.

Kevin and I left the school gates and Kevin

headed left, which was a different way to our normal way home.

'Where are we going?' I asked.

'To Shelly's house,' said Kevin. 'She lives in a small block of flats in West Street.'

I was surprised and impressed. Shelly had been coming to our house for ages, and I didn't know where she lived. Kevin had only been with us for a few days and he seemed to know everything. It struck me that my cousin was potentially a danger to national security.

We walked towards West Street.

'What are you going to actually do to get hold of her phone?' I asked.

'I'm going to mug her,' said Kevin.

I didn't hesitate. I turned and began walking back the way we'd come.

'Where are you going?' asked Kevin.

I turned on him, shocked. 'If you think I'm going to be part of a mugging, you are very much mistaken!' I told him firmly.

'It's not a real mugging,' defended Kevin. 'I'm going to wait until I see her walking home, and then I'm going to rush past her and accidentally bang into her. When she drops her phone, I'll apologise, pick it up, and then hand her Krystal's.'

'How do you know she'll drop her phone?' I demanded.

'Because girls always have their phones in their hands,' said Kevin. 'They walk along texting or making phone calls.'

I mulled it over. What Kevin said had a certain amount of truth to it. 'And what am I expected to do?' I asked.

'Your job is to hang around in case it goes wrong,' said Kevin. 'Say she gets angry and grabs me. You come and rescue me.'

I shook my head. 'Shelly won't grab you,' I assured him. 'She's not like that. That's what my sister would do. Shelly's kind and gentle.'

'Then it's strange that she's going out with Banger,' commented Kevin.

I had to agree, it was strange. I also worried that, although Kevin's plan sounded easy and straightforward, when it came to putting it into practice, I was sure things were bound to go wrong.

CHAPTER 25

They did.

Kevin and I arrived outside the flats where Shelly lived.

'She should be home within the next few minutes,' he said. 'We'll hide just round the corner of her block and I'll run out when we see her.'

I followed him to the side of the block of flats and we peered round the corner to watch for her. Sure enough, Shelly arrived, but stomping along beside her was Banger!

'This is a disaster!' I groaned. 'We'll never get that phone off her with Banger!'

'We have to,' said Kevin. 'This is our only chance. And look, just like I said, she's talking on her phone!'

She was, too. Chattering away on her mobile

as she and Banger walked along. Once again I wondered at the idea of Banger and Shelly going out together. It was like seeing a real life version of Beauty and the Beast.

'It's too dangerous …' I said, but found I was talking to myself. I realised with horror that Kevin had already run out from our hiding place and was running full pelt straight towards Shelly with his head down. I closed my eyes and waited for the crash.

'Oi!'

I opened my eyes again. Kevin was dangling in the air, Banger's great fist holding him off the ground. Shelly was still talking on her mobile phone.

'You nearly hit my girlfriend!' growled Banger. 'I'm gonna teach you a lesson!'

Poor Kevin. He struggled and wriggled, trying to bump against Shelly in some way, but Banger held on grimly to his coat as he walked off, still holding Kevin up in the air. I groaned to myself. Now I had no choice. It had to be me who did it! But first, I

had to get hold of Krystal's phone from Kevin so I could do the switch.

I ran out from hiding and yelled, 'Kevin!'

My shout startled both Banger and Shelly, who turned and looked at me in surprise. For a split second I hesitated, realising I was putting my life in serious danger, but there comes a point where you know you've got to do what you've got to do. As Banger, Shelly and Kevin stared at me, I rushed towards Banger and started slinging punches at Kevin, but being careful to make sure that none of them actually hurt him.

'How dare you bash into my friend Banger!' I yelled. 'I've told you to be careful!'

Kevin was stunned, and then he realised what I was up to and as one of my 'punches' 'hit' him, he let me sneak Krystal's phone out of his hand.

During all of this, Banger gaped at me. 'What are you up to, Dickens?' he demanded.

'I'm beating him up for you,' I said. 'For nearly bashing into you.'

Banger shook his head, dumbfounded. 'You're mad, you are,' he said.

Out of the corner of my eye, I saw that Shelly had started talking into her phone again. I did a pretend stumble away from Kevin, saying 'Ow!' as I did so, and crashed into Shelly.

It worked. She stumbled and dropped her phone on to the ground. The trouble was, in the crash, I dropped the phone I was holding. And there they lay, two absolutely identical pink and yellow phones next to one another. Which was Krystal's and which was Shelly's? I honestly didn't know. When

I'd crashed into Shelly I hadn't been concentrating on her phone, just on knocking into her and hoping she'd drop it.

'You idiot!' said Shelly. And she reached down towards the two phones, and then hesitated when she saw there were two exactly the same.

Which one was Krystal's? If I got it wrong, I'd blown it for ever and everything would be lost. I had to act fast! Already, Banger was glaring at me very suspiciously, as if he'd worked out that me being there was no accident. I saw him release Kevin and then swing round towards me.

'Right, Dickens!' he snarled. 'I don't know what you're up to, but it's something. And I'm gonna beat you up for it!'

With that he swung his huge fist at my head. I just managed to duck down and his fist sailed over me. As I ducked down I heard a girl's voice from one of the phones saying, 'Hello! Hello!' That had to be Shelly's phone!

I swooped down and grabbed up that phone,

then ran.

Behind me I heard a roar of anger from Banger. 'Come back here, Dickens!'

I didn't wait to talk to him. I saw that Kevin had taken the opportunity of Banger letting him go to run off as well. The trouble was, Banger had decided that *I* was the one he wanted, not Kevin.

I kept running. I've never been a great athlete. In fact, I've never been an athlete of any sort. I usually come last in the school sports, whatever event it is, so I knew that everyone in our class could run faster than me. But right then I knew that I mustn't let Banger catch me. If he did I was sure he'd take the phone back and the whole plan would fall apart.

CHAPTER 26

I ran and ran and ran as fast as I could.

FACTOID:
Fastest Runners
The fastest runners are sprinters who run the 100 metres. The fastest person in the world is Usain Bolt, who ran 100 metres in 9.58 seconds.

Luckily for me the streets were mostly clear as I ran, otherwise I know I'd have been caught, because I'm polite and stop for people, but Banger just barges straight on and doesn't care who he thumps into. On a few occasions there were a couple of people on the pavements, but I managed to steer my way round them. All the time I could hear the *thump thump thump* of Banger's big boots thudding down hard on the pavement close behind me. A couple of times I actually felt his fingers grabbing at my coat and his breath rasping in my ear, but I managed to put a spurt on and just get away from him each time. Why didn't he give up? I was feeling exhausted, surely he must have felt the same!

When I'd started to run I didn't know which direction to go in. My head was in a whirl. But as I ran, I thought it through and realised that if I ran home there'd only be loads of questions to answer, such as, 'Where is Kevin?'

Also, I didn't know how to text because I don't have a mobile, which meant the only person I could trust who did was Paul, so I headed for Paul's house.

I reached the Grove Farm Estate at a speed that Usain Bolt would have been proud of. In fact, if Usian Bolt had Banger chasing him, I'm pretty sure he could go even faster. But all the time my breath was getting shorter and my legs were getting wobblier, and Banger was definitely closing on me. He didn't even waste his breath shouting abuse at me, he just kept running and running.

Suddenly I saw it! Paul's house, just fifty metres ahead! If I could get there I was safe. My head was swimming now and my breathing was agony. There was a pain in my chest and my knees and thighs ached. I was sure I had blisters on the soles of my feet. I gritted my teeth and put on a last effort, but as I did I tripped on a kerbstone and went crashing down.

'Got you!' yelled Banger triumphantly.

The next second his huge hand had grabbed me by the back of the neck and lifted me up off the ground.

'Now you are gonna get it!' he snarled. And he pulled back his free fist.

'Edward!'

Banger's gran's voice rang out!

I couldn't believe it! It was like being in a time warp. Once again, just like the previous day, Banger Bates was holding me with one hand and about to bash me with the other, when his gran stopped him.

'Put that boy down at once!'

Banger hesitated, then scowled and put me down. Banger's gran joined us.

'Why, it's Dave Dickens again!' She chuckled. 'Every time I see you lately Edward's got hold of you.' Then her smile faded and she turned to Banger and demanded suspiciously, 'I hope you weren't going to hurt Dave?'

'No, Gran!' blustered Banger. 'We were just playing.'

'Cops and robbers,' I agreed.

Banger's Gran shook her head. 'I'd have thought boys of your age were too old to still be playing cops and robbers,' she said. 'Anyway, come in, Edward. I told your dad I'd make tea for you. You can help me peel the potatoes.'

FACTOID:
Potatoes
The potato originally came from South America, and was introduced into Europe by the Spanish in 1536.

'But …' protested Banger, waving his arms about. Banger's gran fixed him with a firm look.

'No "buts", Edward!' she said. 'You're helping me peel the potatoes, and that's that.'

And then she grabbed him by the hand and led him towards the end of the street, and the Bates' house, which was just round the corner.

I didn't hang around, just in case Banger persuaded his gran to let him go. I rushed down Paul's path to his house. Paul opened the door for me as I got there.

'I saw you and Banger!' he said. 'I was going to come out and rescue you when I saw his gran turn up and do it. Did you get the phone?'

I was too out of breath to say anything. I just

pulled Shelly's mobile phone from my pocket and held it out to him.

'Great!' he said. 'And now we know that Banger's gone home, we can safely pretend to send him a text from Shelly!'

With that, he set to work, his fingers tapping out a message on the keypad. When he'd finished, he let out a nervous sigh.

'Now,' he said, 'we just have to wait.'

We didn't have to wait long. Paul had sent a text saying *Dd u mak thos kids at skool sick? U r so cool!*

And Banger texted back: *Yo.*

'Great!' I said. 'That's a confession!'

'It's not enough,' said Paul, shaking his head. Once again he tapped out a message on the keys, and sent it. It was another few minutes before the reply came back, because this time it was longer.

No, not skool dinners. Me did it. Me got them be sick. Me cool.

I was surprised that Banger had written this

much. For him, it was almost a novel.

'Yesss!' said Paul, delighted. He grinned from ear to ear. 'Now to send this on.' And he started tapping the keyboard and touching the screen. As I watched him, I thought once again that I'd ask my dad and mum if I could have a mobile phone. As far as I'm concerned, my brain's grown as much as it already can. And having a mobile phone and knowing how to work it is Science! If I'm going to get a job as a scientist, I need a mobile phone!

'There!' announced Paul. 'I've sent it to Mrs Nelson, Miss Moore and Miss Walcott's email address.' He gave a satisfied smile. 'If that doesn't do the trick, I don't know what will!'

There was just one last thing for me to do and that was to return Shelly's phone to her. I went back to her flat, but Shelly refused to come to the door when she heard it was me calling. So I told her mum I'd accidentally picked up Shelly's phone when we bumped into each other in the street,

and I'd brought it back. Her mum went and got
Krystal's phone off Shelly and we swapped them
over, and then I went home.

CHAPTER 27

Luckily for me, Kevin had decided to lie in hiding so that we could walk into the house together, so I wouldn't get in trouble for leaving him on his own. He'd chosen to hide in Fred's kennel so he could be undercover without being seen. The only problem with this was that it coincided with Fred having a resurgence of his wind problem, so by the time I arrived home and Kevin emerged from the kennel, Fred's powerful farts had contaminated his clothes, his hair, everything about him; which meant that as we walked into the house Dad and Mum both recoiled from the smell that came off him.

'Wow!' croaked Dad, his eyes watering. 'What's that smell?'

'Methane,' said Kevin cheerfully. 'We were doing

experiments at school. It was great!'

And then he went upstairs to have a shower and wash the smell off.

Next morning, it was all over. As Kevin and I walked into the playground, we saw Mrs Nelson, Miss Moore and Miss Walcott standing together by the gates, with very serious and determined expressions on their faces. As Banger arrived for school, they grabbed him and whisked him off to Mrs Nelson's office.

When school started, Miss Moore was back with our class, but Mrs Nelson stayed in her office with Banger. While we were in assembly, I saw Banger's dad arriving, looking puzzled. About half an hour later I saw him leave, this time looking furious.

Banger spent the time up to breaktime with Mrs Nelson in her office, and then returned to our class. He didn't speak to anyone for the rest of the day and his face had just two expressions: misery and an angry glare. But he didn't do or say anything. He didn't even bother to threaten me.

At lunchtime I saw him with his mobile phone, obviously texting, and he looked pretty annoyed as he did it.

The mystery of who he'd been texting was answered at home that evening. Me, Mum, Dad and Kevin were sitting watching the local news on TV – Krystal was still sulking on her own in her room – when there was a ring at the doorbell. I got up because I already knew that the TV reporter was putting Paul's mum in the clear. As I opened the door, I could hear her saying, 'The recent outbreak of supposed sickness at Olaf Smith Junior School has now been revealed as a practical joke played by one of the pupils …'

Shelly was standing outside on the step. 'Is Krystal in?' she asked.

She looked like she'd been crying. Her eyes were all red and puffy.

'She's upstairs,' I said.

Shelly went past me and upstairs, and she knocked on the door of Krystal's room.

'What?!' snarled Krystal.

'It's me,' said Shelly. 'Shelly.'

There was a pause, then Krystal's door opened.

'What?' demanded Krystal menacingly. And then she obviously saw as I had that Shelly had been crying, because her tone softened and she opened her door wider, and Shelly went in.

I know eavesdropping is wrong, but I was worried in case Shelly said anything bad about me to Krystal, like what had happened with me taking her mobile phone. If she did, then it would be time for me to pack my bag and leave home for a bit until Krystal's rage subsided.

I crept upstairs and put my ear to Krstyal's door.

Shelly was crying again, and in between hiccups and sobs I heard her say, 'He told me I was useless! He blames me for getting him in trouble! He said I sent him a text and he never wants to see me again.'

Then I heard Krystal snort, 'Boys! They're no good, any of them!'

Then Shelly asked, 'Can we be best friends again?'

And Krystal said, 'We're always going to be best friends.'

I didn't hear the rest, because Mum came out of the living room and called up, 'Dave! What are you doing up there?'

'Nothing, Mum!' I called back. 'Just going to the toilet!'

So that was that. Paul's mum's job was saved, Banger was revealed as the culprit behind the mystery vomiting, and Krystal and Shelly became best friends again; so life returned to normal. It also turned out that Banger's dad didn't know anything about what Banger had been up to; he genuinely thought that Banger had been made sick because of the school dinner.

There was one last thing. A couple of days after all this, Aunt Brenda turned up, back home from Turkey, to collect Kevin. She was on her own.

Kevin and I were in my room when we heard her arrive.

'Kevin!' called Mum. 'Your mum's here!'

'Looks like it's time for me to go,' said Kevin, and he picked up his bag, which he'd already packed. But he didn't go straight downstairs. Instead, he stayed on the landing and listened to our two mums talking downstairs. I listened with him.

'Where's Brian?' asked Mum.

'Huh!' snorted Aunt Brenda. 'Don't talk to me about that louse!'

'What?' asked Mum. 'Why? Did the Turkish police release him?'

'The Turkish police did, but they deported him back to England because he's wanted over here. So he's now in jail awaiting trial.'

'What for?' asked Mum, stunned.

Kevin turned to me, a look of triumph on his face. 'A serial killer!' he mouthed. 'I told you!'

'He's a con man who preys on lonely widows and divorcees and takes their money,' said Aunt Brenda. 'I hope he goes to prison for a long, long time.'

Kevin shrugged. 'Well, I was nearly right,' he said. 'Con men's ears are very similar to serial killers'.'

After Kevin had gone, I took Fred out for his walk.

'Well, that's Kevin gone, Fred,' I told him. 'Our house can return to normal again.'

Fred wagged his tail happily, as if he understood my feeling of relief. But I had to admit that Kevin had played a big part in solving the crime over the vomit. The house was going to be quiet without him.

'We've got our lives back, Fred,' I said. 'We can do the things we want to do again, without worrying that Kevin will get us in trouble in some way. The world is ours again!'

Fred gave a little happy 'Woof' and farted. Things were back to normal.